False Notes

Tara Manderino

Whimsical Publications, LLC

Florida

False Notes is a work of fiction. Names, characters, and incidents are the products of the author's imagination and are either fictitious or are used fictitiously. Any resemblance to actual events or persons, living or dead, is entirely coincidental.

To purchase the authorized electronic edition of *False Notes*, visit
www.whimsicalpublications.com

Cover art by Traci Markou
Editing by Brieanna Robertson

Published in the United States by
Whimsical Publications, LLC
Florida

ISBN-13: 978-1-936167-37-1

Printed in the United States of America

Simon anticipated the youth coming past the hotel at some point.

When it hadn't happened in the next few minutes, Simon resigned himself to the fact that he would simply have to go looking. Then, she made an appearance. It just wasn't quite the appearance he expected. When he heard loud voices coming clearly from down the street, he turned in that direction, ready to deal with whatever came his way.

In the semi-darkness, he couldn't make out the figures, but there seemed to be plenty of action behind the saloon doors. He stood on alert, straining to hear the words. Deciding he would have to move closer, he stayed in the shadows of the buildings, and steadily made his way to the voices. No matter how interesting the youth or how much he wanted to pursue that mystery, he couldn't lose sight of why he was in town—to check on Gregory Weldon and follow the trail of counterfeit money that seemed to surface in Hobart.

"Told you before, you whelp, no matter how much money you bring to the table, it's not going to be enough. Now, scat."

"I need that information, Mr. Weldon."

Simon's brows snapped together. He knew that husky voice. Great, they were tangled together, the youth and his number one suspect. The youth's bravado made Simon break out in a sweat. He, or as he strongly suspected, she, was no match for the man confronting her. Weldon's voice, if that was who was speaking, was deep and rough, sounding as if it belonged to a much older man.

"I told you I would pay anything for it." Now Simon's ears pricked up for an entirely different reason. Those were the words of a desperate person. Perhaps they really were tied together! That's what he was here to find out. He pushed away any preconceived notion he might have had that the youth was innocent. He knew that neither age nor gender would have anything to do with a person's acts.

Not a full moment later, there was a scuffle, and then the youth was practically thrust through the saloon doors. He stumbled, but before he could recover his balance, Simon came up behind him from the shadows and covered his mouth, grabbed him by the arm, and dragged him around the side of the building. The youth struggled to gain foothold on the walk.

Definitely a female, Simon thought, grinning to himself. No self respecting boy would fight that way. He locked one of his arms around both of hers, just below her elbows to still her. She still tried to kick him, but with his feet braced wide, she had a difficult time finding a target. "Hold still," he whispered into her ear when it was close enough. "I'm not going to hurt you."

She slowed her thrashing but still struggled against him. When he made no untoward move, she stilled, looking at him warily from the corner of her eye. He could hardly blame her for that.

"I overheard you out there, and I have some questions." He spoke softly so that his voice wouldn't carry. She pulled against him, but he held her easily. "It sounds as if you're in trouble. Are you?" When she made no response, he gave her a little shake. "Are you?"

Finally, she shrugged her shoulders.

He bit back a grin. Stubborn thing. "Perhaps we can help each other out."

She stiffened in his arms, then started to thrash about, nearly slipping through his hands. He tightened his grip and brought her back hard against his chest. "Just listen before you make any decision." There was no response. "Will you do that much?"

At least he got a very reluctant nod that time.

"Fine. Now, I'm going to remove my hand, but I expect you not to scream. Got it?" Again, a hesitant nod. "Now you can lead me somewhere where we can talk."

Slowly, he removed his hand and she looked at him warily, but she didn't scream.

"How do you know I won't lead you somewhere you can be killed?" her voice whispered in the dark.

Simon lowered his hands. There was always that possibility. "I trust you," he said. "All I want is to talk, and from something you said, I think you can help me. We can help each other," he amended at her cautious look.

Acknowledgements

To my beloved husband, Anthony, who put up with historic railroad timetables and track routes when all he wanted was the current Amtrak schedule!

To Chris and Aaron, for putting up with not knowing what century their mom was in, and as always, to my parents for encouraging my writing habits.

Chapter One

1874

Simon patted his coat pocket again and heard the satisfying crinkle of the telegram. He had waited over a week to hear from Luke. Earlier reports hadn't exactly painted Hobart as a hive of social activity, but Simon was sure it beat Flatwood, where he had been waiting. Patting Barr's Pride on the nose as he walked alongside his horse, he thought patience was not exactly his virtue. He had been in the saddle the better part of the day and, now that he was on the outskirts of town, it was a good chance to stretch his legs a bit.

The night was clear; he swore the stars were only inches from his head and he only had to reach out a finger to touch them. It was one of the things he so enjoyed about the territories. He had no complaints when assignments took him this far west, although he knew a lot of the other government agents didn't care for the area, or the people. They weren't civilized enough, he often heard. He snorted aloud at that; the people he had encountered were a lot more civilized than their eastern counterparts. And that included the Indians. When his horse snorted back, he chuckled and reached over to pat the horse's neck. "You agree, I see."

He put one booted foot in the stirrup, started to heave himself into the saddle, and then stopped, his right foot still touching the ground. He cocked his head to the side, listening again for the sound, and sure enough, it came—a slight scraping noise. When Pride turned his head, as if questioning just what Simon intended to do, he pushed aside the big horse's head and removed his left foot, then quickly and quietly looped Pride's reins around the nearby hitching post. Rubbing the horse's nose, indicating that he should be quiet, he swiftly pressed himself up against the wooden wall of the building and into the shadows, trying to gauge the direction of the sound. There was nothing sinister about it, but it was out of place. Finding what didn't belong was part of his job.

No one seemed to be coming along the narrow sidewalk. Even the doors to the Golden Slipper Saloon were still and looked as if no one had gone through them for the past several hours. Shrugging at his own imaginings, he walked toward the post, his boot heels making little sound on the dusty street. When he bent to release Pride's reins, he stilled as he heard it again. This time, the scraping noise was followed by a loud thump and what sounded like a muffled curse.

Patting Pride on the nose and raising a finger to his lips, as if the horse would understand him, Simon moved back into he shadows of the house and followed the sound. When he found the source, he stood there watching in amusement.

Evidently, the youth was thinking of sneaking out of— Simon glanced at the sign on the porch—KATE's without paying.

He turned his attention back to the youth and stood there, watching as the boy dangled from the second story window, his fingers gripping the windowsill and his booted feet scraping against the side of the house. From where Simon stood, he could hear the youth take a deep breath, and knew he was going to let go. The kid probably wouldn't get hurt, but he sure would make a racket when he landed in the bushes below the window.

With a sigh, he moved below the youth and grabbed hold of his leg. There was a gasp and quick inhalation of breath. Instantly, the youth stilled against the building. Simon felt more than actually saw when the kid looked down at him.

Shooting what he hoped was one of his more friendly grins, Simon raised his finger to his lips, indicating silence, then waved the youth down.

Moving his hand up to the boy's thigh for better support, he was surprised to feel how slender he was. The youth went as still as a statue, and then let go of the window ledge. Simon caught him neatly, steadied him on his feet, and was pretty darn sure this was no lad. He reached out a hand to brush him down, and had his hand slapped for the trouble.

"I'm fine."

Simon cocked his head to one side, looking the boy over, but was sure the youth couldn't see the action in the dark. "You're sure?"

"Positive."

The false husky note had Simon's lips twitching. And, definitely, his attention caught. Why ever would a female be climbing out of the local brothel? Was she looking for something on the side, and if so, why was she dressed as a male? Definitely intriguing. And one thing Simon loved was a mystery. Wouldn't be in his line of work if he didn't.

So, nodding, he let the youth proceed. A moment later, he was following him, careful to stay in the shadows. What on earth was the kid up to? He, or she as he suspected, headed toward the main street, moving a lot more slowly than Simon would have anticipated. He was half-tempted to follow further, but he'd told Luke he would be at the hotel at eight, and it was close to that now. With true regret, he headed back to his horse. He definitely wanted to know more about that youth, but he wasn't here on his own time.

Releasing Pride's reins from the post and gathering them in his hand, he led the horse past the next few buildings to the Grand Hotel. Looping the horse's reins over the hitching post, he took his saddlebags from the animal, tossed them over his shoulder and headed in. The outside didn't look like much, but the inside looked a sight better than many of the other hotels he had stayed at. Here, at least, there was carpeting, and what he could see was in good condition. The windows were clean, and a quick glance at the desk clerk showed he was dressed fashionably. Walking over to the registration desk, he gave his name.

"I don't recall seeing you about these parts before," the clerk told him, peering at him over the top of his glasses.

Simon b t back a smile. In these small towns, it wasn't unusual for even the transients to be recognized. "No, no. Taking a break from all work and looking for a friend of mine. He started a business about here."

The manager's expression smoothed. "You must mean

Luke Hayden. Started a mercantile down the road." He pointed to the left. "Old Sam retired a bit ago so people started going into Pine Grove. It's not too bad of a trip now, but once winter sets in, it will be murder. We're all glad to see your friend here. Helps the town to grow."

The registration book lay open on the wooden counter and Simon turned it toward himself. When the clerk dipped the pen in the inkwell and handed it to him, Simon signed his name.

"That it does," Simon said, accepting the key the man had retrieved from behind the desk.

Simon looked about the foyer, checking to see who belonged and who didn't. There were a few neatly dressed couples, and a few cowhands.

"Lookin' for something?" the man in the hat with the sweat soaked band asked as he sauntered over to the desk.

"Just the stairs." Tossing his key in the air and catching it, he headed for the steps. Inside the room, he turned on the gas lamp and quickly glanced around in a cursory safety check as he tossed his bag on the bed and his hat on the dresser. Rolling his sleeves back, he poured water from the waiting pitcher into the basin and washed his face and hands.

Picking up the towel on the side of the washstand, he patted his face dry as he walked back to the dresser. Running his hand down his angular jaw, he peered at himself in the mirror, making sure that the black stubble of his beard was still presentable. It amazed him that his eyes still looked blue. After all of the dust he had encountered on the way in, he expected the color to be obliterated.

Scoffing at his own absurdity, he rubbed the towel over his eyes, wiping away the dust that had settled in the corners. His sisters often teased him about his thick, black eyelashes, but he assured them they were good for blocking dust. Tossing the towel on the edge of the washstand, he unrolled and fastened the sleeves to his shirt and slipped on his jacket. Grabbing his hat from the dresser, he locked the door and headed back down the stairs, settling his hat on his head as he did so.

Outside, he leaned against the post, watching the comings and goings of the few town folk out at that time of the evening. Of Luke, there was no sign. It had been several weeks since Luke had come to town and set up cover, but aside from a few sparse telegrams, there had been precious little news from him. Simon was getting a little tired of sending that same report to Washington.

Lighting a cheroot, he waited. Briefly, he wondered if the youth would still be in the area, but doubted it. He, or she, seemed to have a distinct destination in mind.

"Still smoking those wretched things?" His friend greeted him as he came up the sidewalk.

Simon straightened, clenched the cheroot between his teeth and extended both hands to his partner. Only an inch shorter than Simon's own six-foot frame, the men met at eye level, but while Simon was compactly built, Luke was somewhat heavier. "Where's your bag?" Luke asked, looking about.

"I already checked in. I didn't want to impose on you too much," Simon said. It would have been no imposition, but it was better to say these things aloud in case someone had reason to remember them later.

Luke nodded in understanding. Then, clapping his hand on Simon's shoulder, he said, "Let me buy you dinner!"

Aside from turning into the thump on the shoulder to avoid being tossed over, Simon hadn't moved. "I'm waiting for someone." That was partly true; he had hoped to see the youth come by. It was possible that she had already passed. Surprised at his own sense of disappointment, he turned his attention to his partner.

"Already? Simon, you haven't been in town for twenty-four hours, have you? Who in the hell do you know beside me?"

Simon stubbed out the cheroot and shot his friend a smile. "No one yet, but someone just happened to drop in on me as I was walking by."

Luke raised his eyebrows in surprise. "Intriguing." He turned to lean against the post, along with Simon.

"Oh no, off you go," Simon told him as he pushed against him. "This is my mystery. You were sent here to deal with a bigger one."

Luke stepped away from the railing, put his hands in the air and chuckled. "If that's the way you want it. Remember, the offer for dinner still stands. And if not dinner, lunch. I'll be waiting at the Grand."

Only Simon would have picked up the undertone in his friend's voice, and nodded agreement. It was Luke's way of telling him that if he didn't see him at one meal, he would expect him at the next. If he still didn't see him, he would come looking.

Simon anticipated the youth coming past the hotel at some point. When it hadn't happened in the next few minutes, Simon resigned himself to the fact that he would simply have to go looking. Then, she made an appearance. It just wasn't quite the appearance he expected. When he heard loud voices coming clearly from down the street, he turned in that direction, ready to deal with whatever came his way.

In the semi-darkness, he couldn't make out the figures, but there seemed to be plenty of action behind the saloon doors. He stood on alert, straining to hear the words. Deciding he would have to move closer, he stayed in the shadows of the buildings, and steadily made his way to the voices. No matter how interesting the youth or how much he wanted to pursue that mystery, he couldn't lose sight of why he was in town—to check on Gregory Weldon and follow the trail of counterfeit money that seemed to surface in Hobart.

"Told you before, you whelp, no matter how much money you bring to the table, it's not going to be enough. Now, scat."

"I need that information, Mr. Weldon."

Simon's brows snapped together. He knew that husky voice. Great, they were tangled together, the youth and his number one suspect. The youth's bravado made Simon break out in a sweat. He, or as he strongly suspected, she, was no match for the man confronting her. Weldon's voice, if that was who was speaking, was deep and rough, sounding as if it belonged to a much older man.

"I told you I would pay anything for it." Now Simon's ears pricked up for an entirely different reason. Those were the words of a desperate person. Perhaps they really were tied together! That's what he was here to find out. He pushed away any preconceived notion he might have had that the youth was innocent. He knew that neither age nor gender would have anything to do with a person's acts.

Not a full moment later, there was a scuffle, and then the youth was practically thrust through the saloon doors. He stumbled, but before he could recover his balance, Simon came up behind him from the shadows and covered his mouth, grabbed him by the arm, and dragged him around the side of the building. The youth struggled to gain foothold on the walk.

Definitely a female, Simon thought, grinning to himself. No self respecting boy would fight that way. He locked one of his arms around both of hers, just below her elbows to still her. She still tried to kick him, but with his feet braced wide, she had a difficult time finding a target. "Hold still," he whispered into her ear when it was close enough. "I'm not going to hurt you."

She slowed her thrashing but still struggled against him. When he made no untoward move, she stilled, looking at him warily from the corner of her eye. He could hardly blame her for that.

"I overheard you out there, and I have some questions." He spoke softly so that his voice wouldn't carry. She pulled against him, but he held her easily. "It sounds as if you're in trouble. Are you?" When she made no response, he gave her a little shake. "Are you?"

Finally, she shrugged her shoulders.

He bit back a grin. Stubborn thing. "Perhaps we can help each other out."

She stiffened in his arms, then started to thrash about, nearly slipping through his hands. He tightened his grip and brought her back hard against his chest. "Just listen before you make any decision." There was no response. "Will you do that much?"

At least he got a very reluctant nod that time.

"Fine. Now, I'm going to remove my hand, but I expect you not to scream. Got it?" Again, a hesitant nod. "Now you can lead me somewhere where we can talk."

Slowly, he removed his hand and she looked at him warily, but she didn't scream.

"How do you know I won't lead you somewhere you can be killed?" her voice whispered in the dark.

Simon lowered his hands. There was always that possibility. "I trust you," he said. "All I want is to talk, and from something you said, I think you can help me. We can help each other," he amended at her cautious look.

He hadn't been an operative for this many years and not learned to be aware of his surroundings, yet there didn't appear to be anything out of the ordinary as she led him down the alley he had pulled them into. Still, he had one hand close to the gun in his belt.

He followed her down another block, and then she turned into another alleyway. He grabbed her arm. She stopped immediately and looked at him. "I thought you trusted me?" she mocked.

"To an extent," he agreed. "But maybe you should tell me where we're going. Just in case we get separated," he tacked on after a beat.

"At the end of this alley there is Doc's office. He...he lets me use the back room, sometimes."

Simon kept his thoughts to himself. "Lead on."

A moment later, she entered the back room, and held the door open for him. He stayed close to the door until she lit a small lamp. The room was minute, not small. He felt like a giant in it, although he didn't have to bend his six-foot frame. She closed the door behind him, which put her even closer to him.

ॾ ॾ ॾ

She inhaled the scent of him as she leaned to light the small lamp on the table. Clean. He smelled of horse and leather and tobacco, an altogether comforting smell as far as she was concerned. She brushed the thought aside. He was here for information. At least, that's what he said. She was a bit wary, but there wasn't exactly a lot she could do at the moment.

"So, why the get-up?" he asked.

Her gaze flew to his. It was difficult to see what color his eyes were with his hat pulled low. Even in the dim light, she could see that the hat was of good quality—not one of those five dollar ones most of the ranch hands wore—then, she frowned as his words penetrated, and she remembered to pitch her voice a bit lower. "I don't know what you're talking about."

She was going to have brazen it out. Maybe she could answer his questions in a moment or two and then he would leave. She had wracked her brain on the way over as to what he could have possibly heard that would mean anything to him.

Before she could think to stop him, he swung out a hand and knocked the hat from her head. When she instinctively bent to retrieve it, he reached his other hand toward her chest. She stopped mid-reach, a hair's breadth from his hand.

He scooped her hat off the floor and tossed it on to the small bed in the corner of the room. "Aside from the hair," he drawled, indicating the long, golden brown mane that had fallen over her shoulder when the hat was dislodged, "no man, or boy, would have stopped if I had reached for his chest the way you did."

She felt herself blush and turned her head away from him.

He gave her a moment before he reached his hand under her chin and turned her to face him. "Now, let's start over. Why the get-up?"

She brushed his hand away, then glared at him, not ready to answer.

He crossed his arms over his chest. "Now, we could stand here all evening, or you could talk and I could get on with my night. I am rather hungry, you know."

She instinctively licked her lips.

His eyes narrowed and he looked at her. "Or, perhaps we could talk, then you could change and we could both go to dinner."

"What do you want to know?"

"Let's start with your name." She didn't immediately answer. He drew himself up, gave a brief bow, and introduced himself. "Simon Barr."

She made no response. She didn't know if she could trust him enough for that.

He seemed to be aware of her thoughts because he gave her a slow smile. She wished he wouldn't have done that. He was handsome enough to begin with—a strong jaw, piercing blue eyes and black hair. The smile just accentuated his lower lip and caused a dimple to appear on his right cheek. It was quite unexpected in such a hard man. She let her gaze rake his form, but she already knew how rock solid that body was. She nearly blushed at the thought, remembering how tightly he had pulled her against him in the alley.

"First name, at least," he said easily. "I have to call you something."

"Kirsten." The word escaped before she thought better of it.

"Now, that wasn't so difficult, was it?"

Her lack of response didn't seem to deter him.

"Now, what can you tell me about the man on the street, Mr. Weldon?"

She couldn't stop the shudder that went through her, but he must not have noticed because he didn't comment. Just stood there and waited. She half turned from him; he didn't need to see her face, she reasoned. "I don't really know anything about Mr. Weldon."

Simon crossed his arms over his chest and studied her. "Now...Kirsten. I just happened to have overheard you talking with Mr. Weldon and you certainly gave every indication that you know *something* about the man. I would like to know what."

She didn't have to answer him. She lowered her eyelids, looking about the room surreptitiously. She liked to keep a gun handy, but she had given it to her sister the last time she had seen her. There wasn't much in the room, not much would fit, but the broom was in the corner. If she could reach it and swing it hard enough...

Her startled gaze flew to him when his arm shot out past her face to rest on the chair near her, effectively blocking her reach to the broom.

"Don't even think about it, darlin'," he drawled.

"Wh...what?" She turned her face away from him. How in the world had he known? She knew she had an excellent poker face.

He pointed to the broom with his chin. "Reaching for anything. Now, you answer my questions and we'll be done."

Catching her lower lip between her teeth, she quickly ran through her options. There weren't many. If he hadn't caught her dressed as she was, she would have been the one asking questions! After all, she was a reporter. She still could ask, some small part of her brain reasoned, but there was something about the man that seemed, well, dangerous. She met his look steadily. "You promised dinner," she reminded him.

"So I did, but I think I have to be whole for you to collect." He straightened and crossed his arms over his chest. "Now, tell me about Mr. Weldon."

"Are you a lawman?" She knew why she was interested

in Weldon, but why would he be? When Simon didn't answer, just waited, she found herself telling him. "He's a wealthy rancher out here, one of the cattle barons. His spread is nearly five thousand acres, the largest around here." That information wasn't secret. She would have felt more comfortable if he had answered her question. Would it be better for her, or worse, if he knew that she was Weldon's fiancée, no matter how reluctant?

₴ ₴ ₴

That much, he knew. The real question was, where had the man gotten his money, money that had appeared rather suddenly, and what exactly did he intend to buy with it? And why wouldn't he need Kirsten's? His job was to find out, and this girl just might have the answers he needed, or know where to find them.

"Then what did you need from him? A job?"

"No, not that." She bit her lip as if unsure of what to say now.

Simon wasn't sure he liked the other scenarios he was coming up with. There was no mistaking that Kirsten was a very attractive woman. Weldon, undoubtedly, noted it, but would he take advantage of that fact?

"He's a friend of my uncle's," she blurted out. "Not really a friend, you understand. More of a partner."

A partner in what? This could definitely prove interesting. "I understand, but I don't know where you fit in the picture. I mean, if your uncle owns part of the ranch…" That was something that had not shown up in the dossier he and Luke had been given from Washington.

She waved away the thought. "It's not about the ranch. He told my uncle that something would be for sale, but it is not. And no matter how much money I give him, he does not seem to care."

Now, they were getting to the crux of the matter. Just what did Weldon want to buy? If he were the one making the money, the cost shouldn't be a problem. It would also explain why whatever amount Kirsten offered him would have no appeal. He straightened, but stood between her and the broom. "You know, I think we should go have that dinner. I find that it's difficult for me to think on an empty stomach."

She looked so relieved that Simon almost felt guilty at the thought of his intent to ask her more questions. But that would be later. He hoped that Luke had been able to learn something in these past weeks in spite of what he said earlier to the contrary.

"Now, why don't you get cleaned up?"

"You will wait outside?"

Simon chuckled. "I don't think so. I'll wait right here." He indicated the screen in the corner. "You can get changed right behind that and everything will be fine."

In a matter of moments, she stepped from behind the screen and ran her hands through her hair. "I don't have a brush here," she told him. "Will this be all right?"

He circled the air with his index finger. "Turn around."

She looked at him, but did as he bid, never taking her eyes off him until she had her back to him. Even then, she tried to look over her shoulder.

Behind her, he placed the palm of his hand on her head and turned it forward, then reaching out and gathering her hair, he ran his fingers through it to tame it and deftly braided it. Still holding the braid taut, he reached in his pocket and pulled out a piece of twine, wrapping it around the end. It was a bit long so it made a thick holder. He ignored the thickness and smoothness of her hair beneath his hands. That's not what he wanted to notice. She made no protest after her initial sharp inhalation of air.

When he was done, he grasped her shoulder and turned her about. "All set?"

"How did you do that so quickly? There must be many women in your life."

"A mother and three sisters is a good start," he told her wryly. "And let's not forget the numerous female cousins."

All true, he thought. He wasn't the only one in his family who loved adventure, and as children, they had all roamed the woods for a long enough time that, invariably, one of the female adventurers would have to redo her hair before going back into the house.

He held the door open for her and followed her out.

Escorting her into the hotel restaurant, he looked about for an empty table out of the way of most diners. He would prefer being able to talk without worrying overmuch about eavesdroppers, at least at this point. Spying the table he wanted, he spoke to one of the waiters. He passed Luke on the way, but said nothing. He knew Luke would meet up with him later.

Once seated, Kirsten studied the menu carefully. "I have never eaten in here," she confided in him.

He wondered if that meant she didn't have many gentlemen callers, although he found that difficult to believe. The hotel dining room, like most other hotels, catered primarily to escorted women. Now that he could see her in better lighting, it was difficult to imagine that she could have even thought to pose as a male. Her features were drawn with too fine a hand. He still wondered how she had managed to tuck her long, golden brown hair under a boy's hat. He clenched his hand, remembering the feel of that hair. That was not what he needed at the moment.

"Then I am especially pleased to have you join me."

During dinner, Simon managed to speak a lot about nothing, just enough to keep her entertained and relaxed, although he felt the wine at dinner, and the dinner itself, did much in that regards.

"Perhaps I can help you buy what you need from Mr. Weldon," he said abruptly.

She blinked her large, green eyes once, then again, as if registering what he had said. Using her napkin, she lifted it to dab at her lips. He wished he hadn't noticed that the bottom lip was fuller than the top, or that they were a pleasant shade of deep pink. "I appreciate the offer, Mr. Barr, but I'm afraid I must refuse."

"Must is such a strong word." He leaned back in his seat.

"Nevertheless, it is the one I mean." She kept her voice even. "I would like to be excused now," she said carefully, beginning to push herself away from the table.

Simon hastily stood and assisted her in standing. "Then I *must* walk you to your home."

"No. That won't be necessary."

"Are you going back to Doc's room tonight?" he asked as he followed her to the exit.

She didn't answer him directly. "Really, I am fine, and I appreciate the dinner. I thank you kindly." She started to walk off, but Simon fell into step with her. "At least to the door," he insisted. He was glad he had the foresight to tell the waiter to add it to his bill earlier. He grasped her arm to stop her. "I would like to see you again."

She turned and grinned at him, although it was a tired one. "Yes, I can see that you would still like answers, but I'm afraid nothing will change. Thank you again, Mr. Barr."

Instead of going back to Doc's, she headed home, at least the place she lived. She had never considered her uncle's house home; not like the home she had left with her sister.

When they had first come from Minnesota, she had thought differently; it hadn't taken her long to learn that every house was not a home.

Fortunately, her uncle wasn't about and she made it to her room quickly. She wouldn't allow herself to think of Simon until she was finally in bed, trying to get comfortable. What in heaven's name was wrong with her? She was a reporter by trade, and she had not asked one single question this evening. Instead, she had allowed herself to be interrogated. He had done it skillfully, but it had been an interrogation nonetheless. If she were truthful with herself, she knew it was because she was afraid of the answers he might give. Simon was just passing through. The town got many of the same type of people every day. Well, all right, she admitted to herself, every few weeks, at least. It wasn't as if the town was on the way to anywhere important. What was so special about this man?

℥ ℥ ℥

Once he was in his room, Simon poured himself a glass of wine.

"Did you learn anything?" Luke asked from the comfort of the chair.

Simon shook his head. "Just more questions." He hadn't been surprised to see Luke in his room; he had expected it. He would have thought the man slipping if he hadn't been waiting for him. The two had been partners for some time now and were well attuned to each other's thought process.

Holding up the wine decanter, he silently asked Luke if he wanted a glass. At the man's nod, he poured another, then brought both glasses over to the chair and handed his friend one, then perched on the wooden chair in the corner.

"What do you think of the town so far?" Simon asked.

Luke sputtered and started to laugh. "Me? You came in, what, this afternoon, and you already met a woman and took her to dinner!"

Simon grinned at him. "Interesting story there and we'll discuss it, but do tell me about the town, and what you've discovered about Weldon."

"Most of the people tend to keep to themselves, so that's a bit unusual."

Simon agreed. "Most little towns are delighted to share everything with their neighbors."

"Exactly. But here"—he shrugged—"I don't know, not a whole lot of gossip is going around."

"Maybe not in front of you."

Luke scoffed. "Come on, Sime, give me some credit here."

Simon set his glass on the nearby table. "Just thinking out loud. Do you think the whole town could be in on it?"

"No one would trust a counterfeiting scheme to that many people."

"What if they don't *know* what the secret is?"

Luke finished his wine and set the glass on the small, round wooden table. "Possible, but not probable. I will say that there is definitely something not right here."

"Well, that is why we are here." Simon placed his glass on the table next to Luke's, then stood and paced about the room. "Have you heard anything else from Washington?"

"One message yesterday saying that several more bundles of twenty dollar bills were delivered to the Treasury. They're checking them now to see if they are genuine or not, but the belief is that they are counterfeit too." Luke shook his head. "It amazes me that anyone ever caught it to begin with."

Simon had to agree with that. The forgeries had been so excellent they could have gone unnoticed for a long enough time to do serious damage to the United States economy. Only by the sheerest coincidence had the problem been discovered when one of the Treasury employees received change after a large purchase. Instinct had made him look at the serial numbers on the bills, he later told the director.

"But why suspect Weldon now? Someone had to tip President Grant off. Even the Treasury didn't report anything specific."

Luke stood and joined his partner, staring out of the window into the dark beyond. "It could be the new bank that opened," he said dryly.

"Don't step any closer," Simon warned, his voice low, "but try to get a glimpse out of the window. How many men do you see on that side?"

Luke didn't seem at all surprised at the abrupt change in the conversation. "Three here. You?"

"Two. I'm just not sure if they're waiting for me or you."

"You're much too suspicious," he told Simon dryly. "Could be neither. Take a look at the saloon."

Simon quickly stepped to Luke's side of the window and looked down. The men were still on alert, but Luke was right. They seemed to be waiting for someone from the saloon. Either it was someone who was going to need help, or someone who needed a lot of protection. He was going to find out which.

"I'll be behind the store," Luke reminded him as he watched Simon head out the door.

Chapter Two

As soon as Simon was gone and all seemed quiet, Luke let himself out of the hotel through the back entrance. It wouldn't do for anyone to see that he and Simon were working together. At least not yet.

The two of them had been partners for two years now and knew each other quite well. When President Grant had called them both in to meet with him that first time, Luke had been positive the scheme would never work. Simon, on the other hand, had thought that being part of a secret service to flush out counterfeiters was a brilliant idea. At first, Luke thought he was just playing up to the president. Then he realized that Simon was deadly serious. Of course, the man's confidence was tremendous.

Back in his own rooms behind the mercantile, Luke removed his neck cloth and jacket and set about checking his weapons and store of explosives. One never knew when they were going to be needed, especially now that Simon was on the scene. The man did know how to make things happen! Luke grinned to himself. But then again, that's why Simon was one of the best.

₴ ₴ ₴

Simon slipped behind one of the porch posts close enough to the two men to hear anything they might care to say, but so far, they were being remarkably quiet.

"He comin' out yet?" the one man practically hissed the words to his partner.

"He shouldn't be too much longer. I think he's already won everythin'"

"Good, good."

"Ain't gonna make much difference to you; we still ain't gonna get paid before Friday."

"He gave us a bonus one time."

The other man's whole demeanor perked up. "That's right. He won a lot like tonight, too. Got an extra twenty dollars that time."

This time, *Simon's* ears perked up. Twenty dollars. Just the denomination he was looking for. Now, if that was indeed Weldon inside, which he strongly suspected, he was going to have to come up with some reason to talk to the man. Or, he could wait for the next encounter. He was sure there would be one.

Deciding that, since he hadn't been spotted yet, this would simply be a reconnoiter mission, he waited.

Not long afterward, a tall, heavily built man came out of the saloon.

Immediately, the three men on the one side of the street fell into step with him. The other two waited until he was close and then stepped behind him.

"Mr. Weldon," he heard the one man greet him.

Bingo!

From the shadows, he watched as they mounted the waiting horses and headed out of town. A carriage, he could have followed, but horses, especially since his was in the livery, would be difficult to manage. At least he knew where Weldon could be found. Anyone would have that information if Kirsten was right about the size of his spread.

Staying in the shadows, he made his way to Luke's temporary dwellings and tapped on the door to have it instantly opened.

"Guess they weren't waiting for you," Luke said by way of greeting.

Simon removed his hat and set it on the table. "Seems they were an escort," he said, and quickly summarized what he had heard.

"One night, Simon." Luke held up his index finger and grinned at his partner. "One night and you know it all."

Simon chuckled and shook his head. It was a long-standing argument with them. "I may have learned something, but it's going to take some work to find all of the pieces and tie them together."

"So, who were you having dinner with tonight?"

Simon grinned at him. "Wondered when that would come up." He pulled out a chair at the table and sat, leaning back and draping one arm over the chair's high back. "That was Kirsten."

"When did you have time to meet her, and does she have anything to do with this case?" Luke pulled out another chair and joined him. "Can't recall seeing her around."

"I met her earlier this evening, as she was climbing out of the window from Kate's—er—house"

Luke nodded. "Don't see too many of those girls in the store. They usually just send their housekeeper, Maj."

"I'm not sure if she is one of the girls; she was dressed as a boy and escaping from a window."

At Luke's raised eyebrows, Simon continued. "But the really interesting part came later when I heard her trying to pay Weldon off."

Luke shifted closer in his seat. "Definitely intriguing. What else did you learn?"

"Unfortunately, not much. I do know where she claims to sometimes live, but not when she is really there." Simon pushed away from the table, stood and reached for his hat. "I'm heading back to the hotel and then to Doc's in the morning. I'll stop by sometime in the afternoon."

"What do you need the doctor for?" Concern for his friend colored his voice.

Simon rubbed his shoulder. "I've been having pains here." When he saw the unease on Luke's face, he continued by rubbing his thigh, "...and here."

Luke leaned back in his seat and rolled his eyes. "I guess I'll find out when you tell me."

Chuckling, Simon made his way out of the rooms.

The visit to the doctor's occurred later than Simon expected. First, he had to visit the bank and cash a check issued to him as part of his cover, an unusual procedure on his job, but in this case, very necessary. The inside of the Weldon Bank & Trust proclaimed wealth and establishment. It looked as if it had been on the site for at least ten years, not the four months it had been.

"New here, aren't you?" the teller asked as he handled the process. Simon watched every move the man made without appearing to do so. He performed exactly the same as every other teller had ever done.

"Visiting a friend of mine, Luke Hayden." Simon watched the man count the money a second time before thinking of passing it on to him. He had hoped there would be a twenty dollar bill, but there wasn't. Either it was because he was new, or they saved the larger bills for larger transactions.

"Everyone sure was glad he took over the business, I'll tell you."

"I haven't been to the store yet myself, but plan to head over later."

"You mean he doesn't even know you're in town?"

"He knows I'm here, but we haven't had a chance to visit yet. I thought I would surprise him after I finish my errands."

"You stayin' at the Grand then?"

Simon looked at him sharply. "How did you know that?"

The teller chuckled. "Not hard to figure out. I mean, you're well dressed, so I don't think you'll be staying at Molly's, and that's a nice bit of money there you collected." He cocked his head in the direction of Simon's wallet, which he held in his hand.

Simon gave him an easy smile and tucked the money in his billfold. "Good piece of deduction there."

"We notice things in this town. Now, do you need anything else, sir?"

"No, thank you. I have enough for now." Simon stepped away from the counter, left the bank and headed toward Doc's only to find several people in the waiting room.

Giving his name to the receptionist, he took one of the empty seats. He ignored the few curious glances and leaned his head against the wall, closing his eyes. He hoped they would talk. No matter what Luke said, there had to be gossip.

But there was precious little. The routine chatter about families, but nothing that would mean anything to him. And then it was his turn.

"You look fine to me," the doctor said after Simon sat on the exam table at the man's request and he checked his eyes and throat.

"I feel fine. I need to ask you a few questions."

"Now see here, you're taking time from my patients who need me." The doctor stepped away and busied himself putting his instruments away.

Simon slipped off the table to stand in front of the doctor. "Since I seem to be the last patient for the morning, I don't think that's quite true."

"I don't have anything to talk to you about. I don't even know you." He started to toss the new file for Simon on the desk, then seeming to think better of it, walked it over and put it down.

Simon watched as the man reached for something hidden. It didn't take much to figure out it would be a weapon. Simon was there before him, grasping the doctor's arm, holding it immobile. "I only have a few questions. I don't see there's any need for violence."

The doctor raised frightened eyes to his and Simon smiled, not unlike a fox. "Now, when I release your hand, you're going to turn around and talk to me, right?"

It took a few tense seconds, but the doctor finally released the revolver and nodded in agreement.

Simon moved his hand and stepped away, giving the other man space to move, but not too much. He was used to being in control of the situation and he intended to keep it that way.

"I met a girl last night who says that she stays in the room behind the surgery. What can you tell me about her?"

"I don't know what you're talking about." The doctor lowered himself to the stool by his desk.

"I think you do. I would appreciate some answers." Simon leaned his hip against the man's desk, but gave him enough room so as not to feel as if he were going to be attacked, although Simon would have liked to rip the answer from the man's throat.

"Perhaps you should ask her yourself."

He looked at Simon unflinchingly and his respect for the man grew a notch.

"Listen, Doc, I have some answers from her, now I want some from you."

"What did she tell you?"

"This is getting us nowhere. I want to know who she is and where does she live?" Although he knew the answer, he wanted to know if the doctor would share it. "I have a feeling the room behind the surgery is a bolt hole and I want to know why."

"And I need to know why you're interested." One palm rested on the desktop as he leaned forward.

Simon had to admire the man's tenacity. Either he was related to the girl, or protecting her from something. "How is she related to you?" The man was too young to even suspect she was a daughter.

Doc shook his head and held up his hands. "She's not." He appeared to consider for a moment, then rising, he seemed to come to a decision and told Simon what he knew, which wasn't much indeed. Simon sensed the other man wasn't comfortable with telling him even that much, and at first, he kept the answers very vague, something Simon appreciated.

Simon had paced a bit as the doctor spoke, but finally relaxing, he leaned against the exam table and crossed his arms over his chest. "Look, Doc, I only met Kirsten last night and then she disappeared. I'd like to find her again and am having a devilish time doing it. I thought you could help."

"I can't imagine what you need her for. She's a young girl, and alone. Leave her in peace." There was genuine concern in the man's voice.

Simon raised his eyebrows at that. Kirsten was a very attractive woman. Surely, the doctor had noticed. If the man hadn't been wearing a wedding band, he might have asked if he had been courting her himself. Not that vows or a piece of jewelry would stop some men.

Smiling at the doctor, he said, "Does she have to be alone? I really just want to get to know her better." Even as he said the words, Simon knew there was something wrong with them. He really did want to get to know her better, and not just for the information she might have. That set off the warning bells in his head. This was his case; he had to remember that. But she did have the most engaging smile, and gorgeous green eyes with thick lashes. How had she ever thought she would pass as a lad?

"It's not that I don't trust you, but perhaps you could leave a message that I can pass on to her? That would be best."

Simon gave a curt nod. One thing he was careful not to

do was to leave any more notes than he had to, for anyone. In his business, he had seen too many samples of forgery, and he didn't plan to add to them, so when the doc handed him paper and he indicated that he could sit at his desk and use his pen, he was careful to print out his message for Miss Kirsten. Very few people knew his handwriting and he planned to keep it that way. "I don't even know her full name," he said.

"Bentzer."

Since Doc barely moved his lips delivering that piece of information, making it clear that it was unwillingly given, Simon dropped the matter. He had what he wanted.

Later that afternoon, when he entered the mercantile, there were a number of housewives shopping. He noticed that they gave a bit of room to the woman Luke was assisting. He observed them for a few moments while looking about the shelves himself. It looked like most of the shops in the territories he had been in. There were shelves and counters stocked with a little bit of everything, from lengths of cloth to coffee pots, so at the worst, people would be able to make do until an item was shipped in from the east or San Francisco. The railroad had certainly made life in the west much more livable, Simon thought as he looked at the display of knives in a wooden case.

Luke would let him know when he should be noticed. In the meantime, he did get to hear a bit, just not what he needed.

"I'm telling you, I don't think she's just the housekeeper," the one woman was saying. She didn't bother to keep her voice down.

Simon took another look at Luke and the woman under discussion. She seemed somehow familiar, but he couldn't recall ever meeting her. Her hair was a light brown, almost blonde, and she had long, sandy-colored lashes. The next quick look showed a pert nose and full lips. Simon suspected that she could look quite stunning if dressed properly.

"That's not very Christian," the other woman said. "She might be just as she says."

"Then why would she work at that place? She should find a respectable place to work."

"Isabelle, you know darn well there aren't many places a woman can work out here." She pointed with her chin to

Luke and the woman. "Maybe she'll marry Mr. Luke and that would solve the problem."

Simon gave a quick glance back to the counter. Luke did look interested; genuinely interested. Not his usual "trust me" look.

"No man wants soiled goods."

"You shouldn't spread rumors, Isabelle," the woman said as she stepped away from her friend, and backed into Simon before he could move out of the way.

"Excuse me," she said breathlessly as she turned to face him.

Taking a step back, Simon tipped his hat. "My fault."

"Why, you're new here, aren't you?" She looked up into his face, examining it, as if making certain she hadn't seen him anywhere before.

And Luke said they didn't gossip. He was just about to introduce himself when Luke came bustling over to him, arms outstretched.

"Simon, great to see you!" He thumped his friend on the back, then clasped his right hand. "I didn't think you would ever make it out this way." Keeping an arm around Simon's shoulders, Luke introduced him to the women in the shop who were now standing around them. "This is my great friend, Simon Barr. He's one of the biggest railroad managers back east."

"Whatever brings you out this way, Mr. Barr?"

"Why to check over the railroads, Mrs. Murphy," Luke answered for him.

"Just how old are you, Mr. Barr?"

Simon chuckled. "It's not polite to ask a man his age, ma'am."

The other women tittered and the one patted him on the arm in a motherly fashion. "Maude here is one of the biggest matchmakers in the territory," she said, "and since you aren't wearing a wedding band, she figures you're fair game." She was also much younger than the other women present by a good twenty years.

"Well, I don't know..."

"Nonsense," Maude said, seeming to have recovered. "There's going to be a dance over at the grange tonight. We'll expect your friend to drag you there if he has to." She shot a coy smile at Luke.

Simon bit back a laugh, turning it into a cough. "I'm sure we'll be delighted, ma'am."

After the women left, Simon turned toward the counter only to see that the woman Luke had been talking to earlier was also gone.

"Didn't you want to introduce me?" Simon leaned one elbow on the counter and used his chin to point in the direction of where the woman had been standing.

Luke leaned against the other side of the counter and waved away that thought. "I didn't want the old biddies to start in on her again. They do every time."

"I heard a bit of that. Do you think they're right?" He practically saw the hair on Luke's head stand out, and he put his hands up, palms out. "Hey, easy. I'm just asking a question here."

Luke ran a hand through his hair and sighed. "I know. But you don't know her, Simon. I know she's telling the truth."

"Interesting thing, that. What is she saying?"

Luke straightened and started to pace behind the counter. "It sounds like something out of a novel."

"Do you think it's a story?"

When Luke stopped to look at him, Simon told him to look at it objectively. "I'm not making any judgments, I'm just asking questions. Hey, I'm on your side, remember?"

Giving him a curt nod, Luke continued. "She claims she's in the area because of her uncle."

"Then why isn't she living with him?" Women in the west had much more freedom than those back east, but it was still inconceivable to him that a young woman with a relative nearby would live on her own.

"She was at one point, but when she got this job they wanted someone to live in."

"And he was all right with this?" It was hard for Simon not to sound incredulous. As a newcomer, he would have guessed that the woman was alone. That could set her up for an uncomfortable life. What kind of man would let his female relative work in such a place? Unless it was as the women had said and she was more than the housekeeper, and the uncle was getting something from it. That made sense. He wouldn't say anything to Luke at his point; he could see that his friend was already wound up over the issue.

Luke scoffed. "Can you believe it? According to Maj, he's all in favor."

"What does he get from it?" The question slipped out. If it had been anyone but Luke, there would have been no slipping. He was so used to thinking aloud around his partner that it came out automatically.

"I haven't found that out yet."

The man sounded frustrated, not offended. Simon straightened from the counter and raised one hand to his chin, rubbing it.

"Okay, looking at this objectively, how does this precisely help our case?"

"Wondered when you would get to that." Luke shot him a sheepish grin.

"Right. Now, about this dance..."

"It's the best place for us to be," Luke finished. "If not to see everyone, at least to determine who's not there."

"Thought you would see it that way." It had taken Simon some time to point out the value of social venues to Luke. "Now, do you want to meet before or at the grange?"

"No reason not to go together now that we've established we're great friends. Stop by after dinner."

That didn't give him much time, Simon thought as he made his way to the hotel. Once there, he asked for any messages, of which there were none. He hadn't known about the dance when he had sent the note asking Kirsten to meet him.

As soon as he put the key in the lock of his room, he was aware something was wrong. The very air didn't feel right. He continued to turn the key with one hand while he used the other to reach inside of his jacket pocket for his derringer. He pushed the door open carefully, and quickly stepped to the side, flattening himself against the hallway wall.

When a shot rang out, he bent double and went into the room ready to meet any attack. He straightened in a moment, aware that the danger had passed. The room was empty. A glance at the window showed it was open. Yet he had firmly closed it before he had left. Walking to the window, he stood on the side and peered out. There was still plenty of light to see, and nothing was moving.

With a sound of disgust, he closed the window, then tucked his derringer back in his coat. The story out was that he was a railroad manager. So, either someone knew who he really was, or someone was after the manager. Interesting either way. Quickly washing his face and hands and donning a clean shirt under his jacket, Simon made himself ready to go back out for the evening.

This time at dinner, he made sure he was seated at a table in an alcove with his back to the wall. He preferred peace and quiet when he could get it.

Even if he hadn't known about the dance beforehand, he would have been drawn to the activity in the street and around town. He had planned to make himself known to all the businessmen in the area tomorrow. After all, the railroad could certainly use their support. But it appeared that he might have the opportunity this evening.

Stopping at the mercantile as agreed, Simon went around the back where Luke had his living quarters, announced his presence and that he would be waiting in front of the store. The better to watch everything on the street. Mostly couples, young and old, were walking to the grange and arriving in buggies, but there were also a few groups of young men on their own. Simon gave a wry smile at their antics in trying to attract the young girls walking with their families.

"Were you ever that young?" Luke asked as he came up beside him.

Simon scoffed. "At that age, I was already in the cavalry."

"Still, there must have been some hijinks there. And I know there were dances."

"I was deadly dull, I assure you."

"Deadly, I believe. Dull, never." He slapped Simon on the shoulder. "Let's go."

Simon didn't see himself as exciting, although he was the first to admit nteresting things did tend to happen in his vicinity. Luke hadn't been stretching the truth much stating that he had been deadly. It wasn't something he was overly proud of, but he had done it in the service of his country. He still did.

They mingled with the rest of the people, and then Luke introduced him to the people he knew, who in turn, pointed out some of the more prominent landowners around. Weldon was absent, he immediately noted.

"So, you're the new guy from Missouri Rail Road," a ruddy-faced man said, extending his right hand. "Jeremiah Jones."

"How do you do, Mr. Jones? I planned on meeting with you, but perhaps we can talk now."

"Meet with me, you say? Why, what for?"

The man appeared almost apprehensive. Simon immediately put him at ease. "Merely for your opinion on the railroad service, sir. I understand you send your cattle over the rails."

He watched the suspicion drop from the man's face. "Exactly so. Twice a year."

"And how have you found the service?" Without appearing to, Simon continually watched the crowd, not even certain what he was looking for. Anything that appeared off kilter at such a gathering would catch his attention. He may not have been in this town long, but the rhythm of all small towns was the same. When it wasn't, there was something to worry about.

Then he saw the woman Luke had been speaking with earlier. Even if he hadn't been convinced by her appearance, he was confident by the wide berth most of the women gave her as she made her way into the room. She stood uncertain, looking about. That must have meant that she hadn't planned on meeting Luke, or did it?

Excusing himself from Mr. Jones, he made his way over to where she now stood close to the wall of the room. She looked as if she would prefer to go through it than deal with anyone present. Most of the men gave her speculative glances while the women they were with looked the other way. She certainly wasn't dressed as if she was a prostitute, but then again, some of the highest paid courtesans hadn't either. Not that she was that attractive, but appealing in her own way. He studied her profile as he walked closer to her. Where was Luke anyway?

Her hair was tightly pulled back and in a neat bun, and her nose titled up... he was certain that he had seen her before, and not just in the mercantile. There was something very familiar about her. To one who made it his business to study people and human nature, he was careful to include their appearance in his mental notes, but he just couldn't place her, even if her appearance did nibble at the corner of his mind.

"Hello," he addressed her.

Apparently, she hadn't expected him to come up to her, or anyone else for that matter. She seemed to shrink against the wall. She looked at him warily before offering a timid greeting.

"Allow me to introduce myself. I am Simon Barr." He leaned in a bit and gave her a slight smile. "I'm a good friend of Luke Haycen's."

She visibly relaxed. "I thought I would meet him here, but I haven't seen him. We talked about it," she hastily added as if afraid Simon would think she was chasing after the other man.

Simon had also lost sight of him, which meant the man was investigating something or other. "He came in with me, so I'm sure he's about somewhere. In the meantime, would you care to dance?"

"Me?"

There was no mistaking the astonishment in her voice. Simon made a show of looking about as if to see if he was talking to anyone else and then his gaze rested on hers again. "Yes." He held out his arm and she rested her hand lightly on it as he escorted her to the floor where they joined the other dancers in the Galop. They had an amazing amount of room around them, he thought wryly.

When the dance was finished, he spotted Luke and escorted her in that direction.

"Maj," Luke greeted her. "I see you've already met my great friend, Simon."

She smiled shyly in response. Still speaking in her direction, but directing his words to Simon, Luke said he had been blowing a cloud with Mr. Riley, then he turned to Simon. "He mentioned you were surveying the railroad service."

"Yes, indeed. And, in fact, I must talk to a few more people tonight." He gave a short bow in Maj's direction, and headed outdoors.

He wondered if Kirsten would make an appearance tonight, or if he should start scouting around. Taking out his pocket watch, he held it to the small bit of light coming from the grange. It was past the time they had agreed to meet, but not unduly so. He walked as far as the hotel, and then leaned against the building, waiting for her to arrive, when the sheriff came by on his rounds. Simon gave him a nod, but the man insisted on coming up to speak with him.

"Saw you come from the grange. Is the music too loud for you?"

Chuckling, Simon answered, "No, it's very good, in fact. I'm just waiting for someone." Extending his hand, he introduced himself. "Going about your nightly rounds, I see. It must make the citizens feel very safe."

"I try my best. These are wonderful folks around here."

Simon looked around the small town street. "My friend, Mr. Hayden, has the mercantile down the street a bit. He has no complaints." Where was Kirsten?

"Fine man, there. Well, I'll be on my way." He held his finger to his hat in a careless salute and sauntered off.

"Is he gone?" Her whispered voice carried on the breeze.

Simon didn't turn around. "Are you hiding from the sheriff too?"

"No." Her voice sounded a bit closer now. "We just don't get on all that well."

This time, Simon did turn and watch as she stepped from the shadows. Even in the dim light he could see she really was a lovely woman, even more so than he remembered. He extended his arm. "Shall we join the others at the grange?" She hung back and he let his arm fall to his side. "I see that is not a good idea."

"No, it's not. Do you suppose we could just go somewhere and talk?"

Talk was good. You learned a lot of things that way, the easy way. "Back to Doc's?"

"No, he has patients tonight. Could we just go somewhere? Behind the hotel, the livery? I don't care, just somewhere where no one will hear me."

Definitely interesting. "My room?"

"No, people will see me go in. Could you meet me in front of the bookstore? We could be looking there and no one will be surprised."

He shifted his gaze from hers and looked down the street to see where the store was. Nodding, he watched her skitter away. There was simply no other word for it. She hadn't looked as frightened as she had nervous. That was puzzling. After all, this was the same girl he had caught climbing out a window at a bordello and challenging Jack Weldon.

"Is there a reason for all this subterfuge?" he asked in a teasing voice when they met in front of the store.

"Yes," she said, then shook her head. "No. I really don't know. And I don't even know why I'm telling you except that you have an honest face, and you did already ask me to meet with you."

He tried not to let the word "honest" rankle. He had honor, but honesty was not exactly what he would say was entailed in his line of work.

"I'm delighted you were able to meet me. For a while, I feared you would not." That was definitely true; there was something about her that he found downright intriguing. And he didn't think it was just the mystery of their first meeting.

"I did think about it," she told him, "but then my uncle rather forced my hand."

"You have relatives around here?" He would have thought she was on her own.

"Relatives I have, but not a family," she said bitterly. She gave him a tight smile. "Excuse me, I did not mean to sound so dramatic."

"But your uncle...?"

She turned and clutched his arm. "I'm beginning to think that he is mad."

This was the same uncle who was a partner with Weldon? "How can I help?"

Chapter Three

She scoffed and turned away. "I don't know there's any-thing you, well, anyone, could do. Or if there is anything to be done."

Simon laid his hand on her arm and turned her toward him. "What is it? You can tell me."

"I don't know anything about you." She did turn to face him.

"And that's exactly why you can talk to me. I don't know anyone you know, so I can't carry any tales. I'm safe." He gave her a benign smile to prove it. "How did your uncle force you leave? I might have to thank him, otherwise you wouldn't have come to me."

"I don't think you'd want to thank him," she said.

Simon looked about him. They were still in plain view of the street. That might make her feel safe, but made him feel terribly exposed. His back to the street wasn't a particularly comforting feeling. The little bit of reflection he was able to glean from the shop window didn't make him feel any safer. Someone *had* been in his room earlier.

"Look, this might be a lengthy conversation. Why don't we go elsewhere? We can go to the grange. Everyone in town is there." Seeing that she looked indecisive, he again laid his hand on her arm and steered her in that direction. "We don't have to actually go into the dance if you don't wish," he told her in a soothing voice. Going to the grange meant that, if nothing else, Luke would be near by, and that was a good thing.

They stopped short of entering the grange hall. She tugged him to a standstill. "I'm not ready."

Simon raised one eyebrow at that. What did she have to do to be ready?

"There will be people in there that I know," she hissed.

Simon gave her a slow smile. "That is the general idea of a dance. You know, to meet new people and spend time with those you already know. What's the problem?" When she didn't answer, he removed his hand from her arm and grasped both of her shoulders.

"Obviously something is bothering you, Kirsten. I told you, you can tell me anything."

She bit her lip in indecision, then nodded once. It was more a case of him feeling her agreement than seeing the action. When he dropped his hands, she started to walk to the side of the grange building, keeping close to the shadows; she waved him on.

Simon did a mental check of the blade in his boot, the one in his sleeve and the derringer in his jacket pocket, and followed. Judging that they had gone as far as he would like, Simon stopped, reached out his hand and pulled her arm. She looked over her shoulder in surprise. "It will be better back here where no one can hear us."

It would also be a place where he was more likely to receive a knife in the ribs—not that he didn't trust her. He did, even when he knew he should be cautious. Simon pulled her close and set her against the side of the building. He ignored her wary look and stood very close to her, kissing distance, and leaned his head toward her. "This is far enough. Now what is the problem?"

She looked at his face, then focused on his lips. She closed her eyes, and then opened them. He sensed the new resolve in her even though she turned her head slightly away from him. He didn't think it was because she didn't want him to see her expression. He sensed it was because she was very aware of him. That was all right as far as he was concerned because he was having a difficult time remembering what it was she wanted to talk about. When she started, she had his absolute attention.

"My uncle has all of these grandiose plans. He always did, but now he tells me that he has the means to make them come true."

If he were Weldon's partner, he could well believe it. Simon forced a chuckle. "Did he win at cards?"

"No, he never gambles."

"All men gamble."

She waved that away. "That is not the issue. My uncle has no more money now than he ever did, but suddenly, he is making plans to go in partnership with Mr. Weldon."

"I thought you said he was already Weldon's partner?" His voice was sharp and grabbed her attention.

"He is, just not as much of a partner as he would like to be. He has a small portion of Weldon's holdings, very small. He's looking to increase the amount of his partnership."

There was no mistaking the bitterness in her voice, but he couldn't go into that now. She wasn't his primary concern, but it was becoming clear that her uncle might well be. "Weldon's in the cattle business, Miss Bentzer. What does your uncle do?"

"That's just it. He knows nothing about cattle. He has always been a printer."

"You don't say?" The evening got much more interesting. "Then why would he suddenly be interested in cattle?"

"I don't know. I do know that he has been making transactions at Weldon Bank & Trust. When I ask him about them, he assures me that it is none of my business."

"There's nothing wrong with working through a bank," he stated, careful to keep his voice light. Nonetheless, he had a feeling it was time to change the subject. He didn't want her to later be aware of how much she had actually told him.

"How long have you lived with your uncle, Miss Bentzer? Perhaps this has always been the case, but you have been unaware of it."

"No. It's not. This is something new. He's evil, Mr. Barr, and I'm more worried than I've ever been."

Hearing movement behind him, Simon leaned in closer, covering her lips with his. This was definitely not a good move, he thought to himself. She was soft against him and her lips softer. She had initially made a sound of protest, but it quickly turned to one of approval. Not good for either of them if what she had told him was true. With silence behind him, he moved his head, but not before covering her mouth with his hand. "Don't be offended. There was someone here and I didn't know how else to stop you quickly enough," he said, his voice low in her ear.

He wished he didn't notice how soft her skin was. He inhaled sharply, trying to negate where his thoughts were headed, and wished he hadn't. It was impossible not to breathe in the scent of her, the faint trace of lemon and sunshine. And after that kiss, if he was not careful, it was one that he would never get out of his mind.

He stepped away from her. "Do you want to go in now?"

She shook her head. "No, it would be best if I get back to my uncle's. I've already been gone longer than I should be. It's just...he was frightening this evening."

Simon was instantly on guard. "How so?"

She patted him on the arm. "I'm just being dramatic, I'm sure." She started to walk away, but he stopped her.

"I insist on walking you back." They walked toward the hotel in silence. When she stopped to wish him goodnight, he forestalled her. "When will I see you again?"

"I have no idea, but I'm around most evenings."

"How do I get in touch with you? Through Doc again?" He was pretty sure he could track her anywhere, but wanted her to feel comfortable with him. When she didn't immediately answer, he said. "If you need me for any reason, even if I'm not here, get in touch with my friend, Luke Hayden, at the mercantile. He'll know where to find me." He grabbed her shoulders, forcing her to look at him. "You will do that?" He surprised himself at how much it mattered. He leaned in and swiftly kissed her, then turned her away from him. He stood in the shadows, watching her walk away from him.

Noting that the street still seemed relatively empty in spite of the fact that people were leaving the grange, he headed back toward the mercantile. Luke wasn't back yet, but Simon went around to the back of the store, removed his lock pick from inside his jacket and slipped inside. He sat with his chair propped on two legs against the wall, and waited for his friend to return. He dozed, but the key in the lock had him instantly alert.

"Simon?" Luke said as he entered.

Before the front legs of the chair hit the floor, Luke had lighted the lamp on the table near the door. "Thought I might find you waiting," he said easily. "Coffee or whiskey?"

"Coffee would be good."

Once he had the coffee on the stove, Luke pulled up a chair too. "So, what did you think of Maj? Beautiful, isn't she?"

Simon nodded. "That she is. But what do you know about her?" He actually felt Luke bristle. He waved away the question. "I mean in relation to this case? Does she know anything?"

Luke ran his hand down the back of his head. "Not that I know of. There's no way she could be involved."

This time, Simon felt the hairs on the back of *his* neck stand up. "Tell me that you did investigate her." His voice had been quiet, but the silence that greeted him was overwhelming. "Luke, we need to know what we're up against!" In his agitation, he pushed the chair from the table and got to his feet.

"All right," Luke admitted. "I didn't do a thorough check on her. I just went by what little people in town said."

"That is not like you, Luke." Simon lowered his voice. They could be in more trouble than they anticipated. In all fairness, he had to admit this was the first time Luke had ever slipped in this fashion. Thoughts of Kirsten flitted through his brain, but he ruthlessly pushed them away. He had questioned her. Walking to the shelf, he pulled two mugs down and set them on the table.

"You're right, Simon. I know it." Luke stood, linked his hands behind his neck and let his head fall back. "I wasn't thinking. From the first moment I saw her... " He straightened, reached for the coffee pot on the stove and poured the brew into the waiting mugs without looking at Simon. "It's like there was a piece missing. She slipped right into it." He put the pot back on the stove. "But it's not too late, you know."

Simon clapped him on the shoulder. "You're right, it's not too late." He hoped. Reaching past Luke, he picked up his mug and raised it to Luke in a salute. "While you were dancing the night away," he said lightly, "I found some interesting information."

"Such as?"

"Such as an uncle supposedly gone mad who suddenly is talking about big schemes—huge, lots-of-money-involved schemes."

"Do tell," Luke said, taking a pull from his own mug.

ㄹ ㄹ ㄹ

The hotel was quiet when Simon had gone to bed, and it was still quiet in the early morning hours as he made his way down the stairs. He only hoped it was early enough to get out to Weldon's before the hands started their work. He wanted to know what really went on at the ranch and the only way he was going to find out was by being there.

He had spent a few moments going over the dossier, provided by Washington, with Luke before he had left last night. There was nothing that could have pointed to Kirsten's uncle, if they had even known the man's name. Yet Kirsten seemed to think the men were working together and what-ever they were working at was not a good thing.

The ride to the ranch was relatively quiet in the pre-dawn light. Ground tying his horse, he slipped in through the east pasture. So far, the map they had of the place proved accu-rate. He scouted around a bit, getting the general feel for the property; it looked like any well-run ranch. Whatever else the man might or might not be doing, he didn't appear to be ne-glecting his supposed livelihood.

Luke had wanted Simon to wait until they had more evi-dence before poking around.

"What evidence would that be, Luke?" he had asked. When the other man didn't answer, Simon shrugged his shoulders. "That's exactly it. We don't know anything. We only have suppositions from Washington that the man is making counterfeit bills."

"Report back here?"

Simon gave him a curt nod. "I should be back well before noon. That will be the busy time in the mercantile, right?"

"Since this is Saturday, more than likely. Why, what are you planning?"

"Why, to send a message. What else could I be plan-ning?"

"What kind of message?"

Luke eyed him suspiciously and Simon found himself chuckling. "A telegraph to interested parties from the railroad manager. Something along the lines of how favorable every-one is of service in these parts."

By the time the sun was beginning to poke through the

clouds, Simon was making his way around to the front of the property and up the drive. The men looked to be well involved in their tasks, and if he wasn't mistaken, Weldon would soon be joining them. All reports had said that the man spent little time in his office, but preferred to be in the field. Simon wasn't naive enough to think that meant no one was in the office.

Riding up to the front gate, Simon was admitted. He made his way to the house, watching the men about their morning tasks. He smiled and waved until he got close to the house and dismounted. No one bothered to stop him, though he was quite aware of all eyes on him. He made it to the door before one of the servants came out to greet him.

"I'm here to see Mr. Weldon on business. Simon Barr," he told the man who had led him into the hall.

He looked about at the artwork on the walls and the stone floor underfoot, and the antique tapestries hanging on the walls. The entire place screamed wealth. Fitting for any cattle baron, he thought.

"Mr. Barr, what can I do for you?"

The man appeared cordial, but Simon noticed the tick in one eye and the slightly apprehensive air.

Simon removed his hat and held it in his hand. "Just a social visit. Since I'm in the area, I thought I would check to see how you, well, everyone in the area, was using the railroad. We want to make sure everything is working to the best advantage for you."

"Oh, indeed. But there was no need to come all the way out here. But since you are here, would you like to join me for breakfast?'

Agreeing, Simon followed him into another room. The entire house, at least what he could see, was done with the same amount of taste and expense. He set about putting his host at ease and listening to all he had to say.

"You're not going to write anything down?"

Simon raised his eyebrows questioningly.

"I mean, don't you want to make sure you have everything for your report? I have nothing but good things to say about the railroad here in Hobart. I would hate for you to mix me up with someone who may not be as flattering."

"Flattering? So, you do have some complaints?"

"Nothing of the sort. Just a word." He waved away the

misconception.

Simon gave him a tight smile as he accepted the coffee that Weldon poured for him. "By the way, I do have excellent recall. I won't forget. Anything."

Weldon's spoon clattered on the saucer, but Simon merely sipped his coffee. Replacing the cup on the saucer, he reached for a roll. "I would be delighted if you would care to show me around."

"Now why would a city fellow like you have any interest in a working ranch?" Weldon shifted his attention to his eggs.

Simon helped himself to his own before answering. "I'm interested in a lot of things, Mr. Weldon, and I've never been on a ranch the size of this one."

Seeming to come to a decision, the man practically preened. "I suppose I could show you around a bit after breakfast, if you have the time, that is."

Simon spent the rest of breakfast chatting about the town. "I even went to the grange last night. They sure know how to make people feel welcome."

"Peasants."

"Excuse me?"

Weldon cleared his throat. "Pleasant. But if you want to see some real entertainment, you have to join us here one evening. If you're in town, that is."

Simon bit his lip to keep from laughing. Nice catch the man made, though. "Perhaps something can be arranged. I do have the railroad at my disposal, you know, so a special trip might be arranged."

The man positively lit up at that comment, and Simon had to wonder why. He was sure he would find out in good time.

"Wonderful. I hold several events here a year. I won't call them balls; that's something for you people back east, but the guests are of the finest families. If you're here through next week when the Cattlemen's Association holds our dance, you could possibly join us. I'll make sure you're on the invite list."

Simon inclined his head in thanks.

"Now, if you're ready for that tour?"

"By all means." He pushed himself from the table and followed his host out doors. He waited near his horse until Weldon's mount was brought around. That gave him an extra few minutes to covertly watch the activity. Nothing seemed at all out of place for a large working ranch such as this one. In spite of what he had told Weldon, he was quite familiar with large ranches and big spreads. He had hoped that Weldon would have included a tour of the office, but that seemed not to be the case. He would have to work on that later. For now, he would learn what he could, which turned out to be not much at all.

If he had needed or wanted the exercise, he wouldn't have counted the morning a total loss. The only thing he was able to spot was that the few men from the card game the other night were indeed Weldon's employees and the one was a foreman. He rode with them, checking the fences along the property line when necessary.

At one point, the fence had separated from the pole in the north pasture. It was noted on Simon's map, so the gap was not a new one, but Weldon treated it as such. For his benefit?

"Well, fix the damn thing," Weldon barked at the man who was already half off his horse and in the process of doing just that.

"Going to need some help here, Mr. Weldon," he said. Reaching into his saddlebag, the ranch hand pulled out his tools, took them over to the post and waited for Weldon to join him. The man appeared to be in no hurry to do so.

Simon slipped from the saddle and ambled over to the foreman. "What do you need me to do?" he asked.

The foreman looked at him, then back to Weldon. Simon followed the gaze and ignored the open amusement on Weldon's face.

"Well, go ahead, Walters. Take Mr. Barr up on his offer. The city boy wanted to know about ranch life."

Simon didn't bother to comment. When the foreman made no response, Simon walked over to the post, setting it straight and tightening the wires on the opposite side. Seeing that Simon intended to work, the foreman didn't waste any time. He grabbed his tools and pulled the down wire taut and attached it to the post.

Simon ignored the sweat dripping down the side of his face until the foreman was done. Releasing the post, he wiped the back of his hand across his forehead and got back in the saddle.

"Not bad for a city boy," Weldon said. "Didn't think you had much cause for fixing fences in the railroad office."

"The Union Army erected their fair share, sir."

Weldon grunted in response and they proceeded about the property It was a large spread all right, and a lot of activity could be hidden in any of the outbuildings, but from what Simon could see, nothing looked out of place. Nothing sounded out of place. Animals were greatly attuned to their surroundings and there were times he knew something was wrong by the animal behavior, but here everything seemed calm, norma .

Leaving Weldon's, Simon headed for town and Luke's. He ignored the two men following him off Weldon's property. Interesting. And something worth exploring later. Right now, he had a telegram to send.

The town was bustling as he made his way in. He greeted several of the men and women that he'd met the night before. Stopping in front of the store, he waited for two women to enter before he did. Thankfully, they weren't the ones who had invited him to the dance the day before.

"Simon." Luke's voice hailed him from the other side of the room. "What can I do for you today?"

Strolling over to the counter, Simon made a show of reaching in h s jacket pocket. "I need to send a telegram to headquarters."

"Don't you just bring the report back with you?" Luke took his time getting out his paper and pencil in preparation for the message. The noise attracted several glances in his direction. "Just let me know what you need to send and it will be on its way."

"Ah, here we go." Simon handed him a piece of paper telling him they needed to discuss Weldon. "Just send what's on that message—that everyone here is downright friendly and approves of the railroad. Oh, and add that I'll be here a few more days."

Nodding, Luke went to the telegraph set up and immediately began punching in the code to their office, letting them know that Simon was in town and planned to remain for several more days.

As Luke sent the message and waited for a confirmation of its receipt, Simon wandered about the store, listening to the women ta k about the dresses and behavior of the others at the dance.

"What did you think of it, Mr. Barr?" the one woman asked. "I mean, you must go to some very fancy dances back in New York City."

"Oh, I do indeed, but I have to say your dance last night had the most interesting company of any I have ever attended."

"Really, Mr. Barr? How exciting."

The other woman practically snorted and addressed her companion while looking at Simon from the corner of her eye. "I don't know. I saw him dancing with that Maj woman."

Simon studied her for a moment, making sure she focused on him before he responded. "One of the loveliest women I have had the pleasure of meeting."

"Yes. Well, one always wonders where men meet such women."

Oh, claws out. "Why, I met her right at the dance last night, in a room full of people. Where else could I have met her?"

The woman blushed, and Simon turned away. Luke had not missed the exchange. Walking back to the counter, Simon handed Luke the amount for the message. "I'll be up for a friendly game of cards," he told his partner. "Think there will be anyone around tonight?"

"Sure to be. This is Saturday night. Hope you can find a *quiet* game."

Simon chuckled. "Feel free to join me later." And he didn't necessarily mean at cards. If he was lucky enough to find a game, he would do his best to glean some information, and that would be worth sharing.

Nodding to the women, Simon made his way out of the store and back to the hotel. As he inserted his key, he heard a slight movement behind the door and stopped. This was getting to be a habit. He knew he had locked the door. Withdrawing his derringer from inside his jacket, he held it ready and pushed on the door at the same time. When there was no reaction, he slipped inside quickly, keeping close to the outside wall. He reached one hand out to turn on the gas wall lamp.

Kirsten sat near the window, watching him with interest. Heaving a sigh, he returned the gun to his jacket and closed the door behind him. He took off his hat and tossed it on the dresser as he walked toward the window. "How did you get in here?"

Her smile tugged at his heart, and he rolled his shoulders as if that would brush it away. This was not something he needed. She patted the folded towel on her lap. "That was easy. I just carried the towels up. I told the desk clerk that I needed to put these in your room."

"And he let you in. Clever." He stood in front of her, making her look up at him. "So, why are you here?" His gaze searched the room. Surely, she hadn't come alone, no matter what ruse she'd used to enter the room. "I thought you didn't want to be seen coming here."

"I wasn't seen. At least, not as me, if you know what I mean."

He had a feeling he knew exactly what she meant.

"I really don't know what to do, Simon."

He was definitely in trouble. He loved the way she said his name. This was not good. He was having a lot more sympathy for Luke.

"I told you about my uncle last night, a little, anyway."

He nodded, encouraging her to continue.

"Today he told me that it would only be a matter of time and everything would be fine."

"What does that mean?" He tried to keep the exasperation out of his voice. So far, she had alluded to her uncle, but really had nothing to say that could link him to the present case except that he was a partner with Weldon. That could be for the ranch only. He planned to wire Washington's data bureau and see what they could find out.

Kirsten scoffed. "I'm not exactly sure, but I am worried. There is no love lost between my uncle and myself, and I'm afraid for when he won't need me anymore, and more and more I feel that could be at any time." She clasped her hands together and twisted them in her lap, looking down at her intertwined fingers instead of at Simon.

"Then why stay with him? Surely there is somewhere else you can go. I'm sure Doc would take you in if you needed a place." He said the words evenly in spite of the wrench to his gut as he did so.

"I wouldn't endanger him." She looked down at her hands, then up again, but she still wouldn't meet his gaze. "Please, Simon, when you leave, will you take me with you?"

In a heartbeat. "What do you mean?"

"Oh!" She blushed and raised her hands to her face, giving a little laugh. "That didn't come out right. I mean, I know you travel on the railroad, and I wondered if you could let me ride with you to another town."

His heart settled back into its normal rhythm. He stepped to the side of her, and stretched his hand out to rest on the wall, supporting his weight as he looked down at the top of her head. "You can buy a ticket at the station any time."

She stood and was closer than he anticipated. When she took a step back, she nearly lost her balance as she tripped against the chair she had just vacated. He caught her close to him.

"I...I don't have any money."

Simon released her and steadied her on her feet. "You were playing cards with Weldon. You tried to pay him off, if I recall correctly. If you were interested in leaving, that money would have taken you to the other side of the country and set you up for some time. So, what are you saying?"

"That wasn't my money," she said. "Weldon didn't take it; I had to return it."

Simon straightened and ran his hand across his forehead. "Would you care to explain that all to me again? Maybe a bit slower since I seem to have a difficult time following."

"No, I can't explain. And I don't think you have a hard time following anything, Mr. Barr."

"Normally, I would agree with you." He crossed his arms. "What if I agree to take you with me? Then what? What will you do? Where will you go? You said you have no family." He wouldn't mind taking her and keeping her, but since she wasn't a stray kitten, it didn't seem a likely option.

"I don't, but I think there are more opportunities for women back east than there are here. I'm a reporter, and a good one."

What she said was true. Not that the opportunities weren't equal. It was just a matter of more need in the east, the need that went with more people.

"A reporter?" She had hardly acted like any reporter he had ever encountered. The surprise in his voice must have come through.

She nodded her head. "I admit that you caught me at a bad time, but I assure you that, normally I would have met you anyway. My uncle likes to have interviews with almost all newcomers to town."

"Your uncle?" The printer. "You work for your uncle?" He posed it as a question, but knew that's what she was saying. But why would that be a frightening proposition for her? Fear was the only reason that he could think that she would need to hide at Doc's. Or secrecy. Did she meet her lover there? Someone her uncle didn't approve of? Simon pushed that thought away. It wasn't a fair one and was an avenue he didn't want to go down. He was here to work on a case where her uncle may or may not be involved, that was it.

"Yes," she confirmed. "Is that a problem?"

"A problem? No, no." Simon rubbed his hand across his chin. "It just took me by surprise. Is there anything else I should know?" He kept his voice light, but sharpened his gaze when she wouldn't meet his and looked away, biting her lip. "You're a reporter. There's nothing wrong with that."

She gave him a half smile. "I agree. I like being a reporter."

"Something gave you concern."

"You asked if there was anything else you should know." She took a deep breath before meeting his gaze. "I'm engaged to Greg Weldon."

Simon's breath caught in his chest. It came out in a whoosh and he tried to cover it with a slight cough. That should mean nothing to him. It meant everything. She could be as involved as Weldon.

She wrapped her arms around her middle. "I need to get away from him." At Simon's skeptical expression, she continued and gave a bitter laugh. "You can't imagine that I would want to be engaged to him! My uncle made the arrangements."

There was definitely more to the story, but Simon took it at face value for the moment. "I would have to let my office know you were traveling with me," he suddenly answered in response to her earlier request.

He watched her face fall; there was no other way to describe it. All the animation seemed to have left it. He realized that she looked as drawn as the first time he had seen her behind Doc's surgery.

"I didn't realize.... I just thought if you were riding on the train, then maybe I could too and not have to pay. I have no, well, very little money, Mr. Barr."

He liked when she used his first name better. Simon took her by the arm and led her to the door. "Let me think on it and let you know tonight. Will that do?" He definitely was going to consider what she said about the money not being hers! Why would she take such a risk?

Once she was gone, Simon flopped on the bed and stared at the ceiling. Everything had sure gotten complicated quickly. He began to think that he was going to have to find out exactly why her uncle was so deranged, or why she thought he was.

There were times he wouldn't change his way of life for anything, then there were times he longed for the simplicity of the cavalry lifestyle. He found it interesting that Kirsten wanted to escape her uncle. He really didn't have time to investigate this small side problem, but he would dearly love to know the hold the man had on her. It had to be more than the fact that she worked for him. He refused to consider the problem about Weldon.

Rising, he washed his face and changed into a clean shirt before heading out to the saloon.

Luke had saved him a spot at the table closest to Weldon's. The man wasn't currently there, but Simon couldn't think of the spot as anything else.

Pulling out a chair, he sat, nodded to the other men present, then he did a double take when he saw Kirsten was in the number. She gave him a sly wink. He wanted to reach over the table and throttle her. What in heaven's name did she think she was doing? Was she trying to raise funds to buy a train ticket? He felt the sweat bead on his forehead and forced himself to pay attention to Luke, who was dealing. How could the other men not realize that she wasn't the stripling she pretended to be? He hoped they wouldn't catch on.

"Stud poker?" Luke asked, shuffling the cards. When he got no response, he tried again. "Five Card Draw?" At the murmur of agreement, Luke began to deal and call for bets.

Simon was in the game, but spent as much time staring at the players as he did his cards. Without seeming to do so, he watched the bills as they made their way to the table. From where he was sitting, the bills looked fine. Of course, they were all small denominations and coins, so it was difficult to determine if they were genuine or not.

"Let's double up, gentlemen." Simon nodded in silent approval. Luke was doing his best to get the larger bills on the table.

The hand went to one of the cowhands from Weldon's ranch. Then, Simon watched in amazement as more and more of the hands went to Kirsten. None of the other men seemed to be aware of that and she was smart enough not to draw attention to the fact. For the next several hands, Simon's gaze never left her, not that she was aware of it, at least as far as he could tell. He studied the cards in his hand. If they were marked, it was carefully done and he could detect nothing on them, and he had seen every variation, as well as created a few of his own.

She seemed to be counting the cards. Amazing that she could track so many. He could do it and he knew several other people, but it was a learned skill. He had a feeling she would do quite well if she did indeed make it as far east as New York. But if she wasn't using her money, whose was it?

Sometime after they had started, Simon found that he wasn't getting a whole lot further than he had been in the morning as far as information was concerned. He excused himself, telling Luke to go ahead and play without him. He could practically hear the man groan.

Leaving the table, he headed outside and waited, but not for long. Kirsten was right behind him.

He let her exit the saloon and then followed her at some distance. Maybe she was going to return the money that wasn't hers. He would love to know where it went.

It wasn't a long walk. She went around the side of Kate's, and stopped under the window she had crawled out of several days ago. Was she going to crawl in? Simon flattened himself against the building, watching her from the corner of his eye.

Chapter Four

Looking around to make sure no one was about, Kirsten stooped down and scooped up a few pieces of gravel near the foundation. There was a light coming from the window near the back, and that's where she aimed her first throw. It took several more before anyone came to the window.

"Meet me around the side," Kirsten said. Her voice was low, not whispered, so that it would carry.

Simon risked a glance, but couldn't make out who she was talking to. Without making a sound, he managed to move and conceal himself behind the building, completely shielding him from her view.

Kirsten looked around. She felt that someone was nearby, but no matter where she looked, she saw no one. Still, it unsettled her. She stayed on the side of the house in the shadows. In another moment, her sister joined her.

"Maj," she whispered from the shadows.

Maj turned from the direction she had been looking. "Where are you?"

Kirsten stepped away from the building, and then hugged her sister.

"What are you doing here? I didn't expect you tonight."

Kirsten nodded, then realizing her sister couldn't see her, said, "I know. I didn't plan on being here, but I overheard Uncle Ralph earlier this evening."

Maj looked her up and down. "Is that why you have those clothes on?"

Kirsten checked her grin. It was no secret that Maj detested the boy's clothing she often wore, but sometimes there was just no help for it. "Exactly why. Uncle was talking to Weldon again tonight and he said that everything should be ready in the next few days."

Maj's indrawn breath sounded quite loud in the night. "I can't let you do this, Kirsten. I...I can't."

Kirsten gave her sister a brief but bracing hug. "It's not really up to you, Maj." It was no secret in the household that Maj had been Weldon's first choice. She still feared that, if Kirsten balked, then her uncle would insist that Maj marry the man. "That's why I went out tonight, Maj. I thought if I engaged Weldon in a game of cards that would mean tonight was a loss to him. He couldn't come for you." He might have been affianced to Kirsten, but there was no denying that Maj held some attraction for him. There had been numerous nights he had come to Kate's and asked for her. Fortunately, Kate was aware of the situation, and made it clear to him that Maj was the housekeeper, nothing more, and it was up to her if she saw anyone or not.

"He probably won't come tonight then." Relief colored her voice. "But that doesn't mean he won't show up another night. This is an impossible situation. What could Uncle have been thinking?"

Kirsten shot her sister a dark look. Her uncle's actions put them all in an awkward situation, and for what, she still didn't know. "Wait." Reaching into her coat pocket, she pulled out most of the stack of bills that she had won that night and pushed them into Maj's hands. "Take this, and use it if you have to."

Her sister pushed it back toward her. "You use it. You may have to buy your way out."

Kirsten gave a delicate snort. "I tried that already and he assured me that I didn't have enough money." She grasped her sister's hand and closed it over the bills. "Use the money to escape if you have to, Maj. Be safe."

Her sister slowly nodded. "But what about you? Won't Uncle take it out on you?"

Shrugging, Kirsten struggled to look nonchalant. She was no stranger to her uncle's temper, but no need for her sister to know that. I'll be fine. He's confident that he already has what he wants."

"Even if he releases you from Weldon, there might be someone else."

"I doubt it. Besides, there is no one else wealthy enough around here to do Uncle any good," she said bitterly. "I won't say he won't try further up or down the river, but for now I think I'm safe. It's you I'm worried about. Now, promise you'll escape if need be, but try to let me know where you are."

Maj gave her a quick hug, then pushed her shoulder. "I think you better get back and changed before Uncle Ralph finds you're gone."

Nodding, Kirsten leaned in to hug her sister again, then stepped away and into the shadows, waiting and watching as her sister entered the building.

Maj might be the older sibling by two years, but Kirsten had always felt responsible for her. Maj was beautiful and needed someone to look after her. Kirsten was well able to care for herself; always had been, at least until her uncle had appeared on the scene.

Even after their parents had died, Kirsten was able to have food on the table for them, always worked at something that would ensure the sisters did not starve. Maj had been the homemaker. Then, their uncle appeared. At first, Kirsten especially wanted to dispute his claim, but he was too much like their mother in appearance and temperament to be otherwise.

In spite of other misgivings, it had not been too bad in the beginning. Then his true, cruel nature made itself known when they moved from Minnesota. He learned that while Kirsten looked like their mother, Maj took after her. She had no desire to help run the paper, or be any part of it, so he had no use for her. The only reason he suffered her as long as he had, he said, was because Kirsten wouldn't let him do otherwise. And he needed Kirsten. He needed someone that could literally run the paper single handedly if he could not.

He had encouraged Maj to leave, and look where she ended up! At least she was still doing honest work, Kirsten assured herself. But when the man felt that he could make a profit by agreeing for Maj to marry the highest bidder, in this case, Greg Weldon, Kirsten knew they would have to get away.

When Maj confided in Kirsten, told her her fears, there

was nothing for Kirsten to do but insist that she be the one to marry Weldcn. Her uncle didn't care either way as long as it was one of them. At first, Weldon had protested, then seemed to come to the realization that it might be a way to have both of them.

Kirsten shuddered at the thought. Maj had to escape, or switching places would mean nothing. Neither of them could figure out exactly how Weldon was involved with their uncle, but knew it had to be something big. Kirsten was confident that she could get away herself if she had to. She had asked Simon to take her, but if he didn't, she didn't have many qualms about stowing away on the train. She would do anything. The thought of being tied to Greg Weldon sent shivers up her spine.

ƨ ƨ ƨ

Simon inhaled sharply. Maj! Luke's Maj and Kirsten were involved in something, but from where he was and the little he heard, he couldn't tell exactly what. That wasn't good. He was going to have to learn more. There wasn't enough light to get a good glimpse of the other girl's features and Simon wasn't sure he would have known who it was if Kirsten hadn't said her name.

He waited until she left, and then he circumspectly followed her. He wanted answers and asking them in a dark alley didn't seem the best way to get them. He waited until she was ready to slip into the room behind Doc's, and followed her.

As she inserted the key, he came up behind her and covered her mouth in one move, not giving her a chance to scream. He did let her see that it was him. He had no desire to frighten her to death; he just wanted answers.

And a whole lot more, he thought to himself, but he kept those thoughts at bay. This was not the time for that. And the way things were going, there may never be time. There was genuine regret in that thought as he let his calloused hands linger over her lips and jaw. "Just open the door," he whispered in her ear. "I'm not going to hurt you."

At her slight nod, he allowed her a bit more room, put an additional inch of space between their bodies, but he suspected that was more for his own benefit than hers. Pressed close he was all too aware of the roundness of her hips and the indentation of her waist. How the devil had she thought she could disguise herself as a boy anyway, and how hadn't Weldon seen it? Not that he was glad the man hadn't noticed. He nearly broke out in a sweat thinking about what the man would have done had he found out.

As soon as the door was open, he pushed her inside, still holding her mouth. "I'm going to move my hand, but no screaming, understand?"

It took a moment, but then she nodded reluctantly.

Simon eased his hand away, and used both hands to hold her shoulders, turning her to face him. He wanted to apologize, especially when he saw the wounded look on her face, but that was the last thing he could do, should do. That would mean he wasn't doing his job, and that had to come first, no matter what.

"I'm sorry about that, but I didn't want to frighten you."

She scoffed at that. "You did a pretty good job of it." She brushed his hands from her, and took a step back, crossing her arms across her chest. "What did you want?"

"I want to know who you were meeting." He wanted her to tell him. It rather surprised him that she did so instantly.

"Maj."

"Why?" She didn't think that was enough of an answer, did she? It told him who, but not why. He had learned to be more cautious over the years. That thought would make Luke laugh, but it was true. He *was* cautious and knew not to trust anyone, ever. Luke was the only person he had put absolute trust in, was the only one who had ever earned it. "I saw you give something to her. What was it?"

"What does it matter?"

"It matters to me. Is it something illegal that you can't tell me about? Who's Maj to you?" He saw the stubborn thrust to her chin and knew he was going about it all wrong, but there didn't seem any way to stop himself. If he let himself go in the least, he was sure that he would believe anything and everything she said, and right now, she was the one lead he had in this bizarre case, or was she?

He wanted to shake his head to clear it. Instead, he reached out a hand to grasp her arm. She flinched, but didn't move. He dropped his hand before he made contact.

"Who's Maj?" He pitched his voice so it was softer and

didn't have the sharp edge from earlier.

"All right"—she gave an exasperated sigh—"but you can't tell anyone in town. Not many people remember. She's my sister."

Simon felt himself relax a bit. He knew that Maj's profile had seemed familiar at the dance. He just hadn't been able been able to place it, but now he realized it should have been quite obvious.

"What did you have to give her at night that couldn't wait until daylight?"

She scowled at him. "Do you mind if I change clothes?" She didn't wait for him to answer, but stalked off to the screen set in the corner of the room and slipped behind it.

Simon wasn't even sure he planned on following, but he had. "I asked a question."

"I don't remembering agreeing to answer." Her voice was muffled as she fussed with her clothing.

He waited a beat. As it was, she was under no obligation to answer him. "You know, perhaps I could help you, if it was something illegal." He hoped to God he really hadn't meant those words that came out of his mouth. "But if there is an innocent explanation, I'm sure you could just tell me."

"Ha! I tried to ask for help to leave here, on your train, remember?" There was a rustle of more clothing.

He didn't think before acting. Women in a state of undress were nothing new to him, not after growing up in a house with three sisters. Single-mindedly, he stepped behind the screen.

When she saw him, she gasped and whirled away from him, covering her breasts, which were already covered by the chemise.

Then it was his turn to gasp as he saw her back. He stepped closer and grasped her arms, hauling her toward him, ignoring her outraged protests. He pushed aside the straps of her chemise. When she continued to squirm, he caught her legs, wrapping one of his around both of hers, stilling her. "I want to see." She jerked her shoulders, but he was intent.

He ran his finger lightly across the welted red scars on her shoulders and upper back. "Who did this to you?" His words were soft, but dangerously so, slicing through the air.

He heard her gulp in air. Knowing that trained soldiers

had been terrified when he spoke quietly, he cleared his throat. He knew he should try to speak normally. He had no desire to frighten the girl, but to think of anyone purposely marring her tender flesh filled him with loathing.

"It doesn't matter. It was a long time ago. Now, let me go."

Simon shifted his weight, releasing her legs, but instead of releasing her arms, he whirled her about to face him. "It wasn't all that long ago." He was quite good at gauging the severity and ages of injuries, he had dealt with his share in the cavalry. "Now, who did this and why?"

She lifted her chin. "I don't have to answer to you."

Simon gave her a tight smile. He suspected that he already knew the answer. There could only be two likely candidates in his mind—her uncle or Weldon. "No, you don't, but you may wish that you had."

Her eyes widened. He could practically smell the fear on her, but she lifted her chin defiantly. Surely, she didn't think that he would harm her? He gentled his grip, but didn't release her.

"Did Doc treat you?"

"No." She cleared her throat. "I had the housekeeper put some salve on the really bad ones."

Simon nodded tightly and grunted, then surprisingly, let her go. The moment he had, he realized she wasn't prepared. She nearly lost her balance with the suddenness of it, but he caught and steadied her before releasing her again and turning away. He stepped on the other side of the screen and paced the small area as he waited for her to finish dressing. It was impossible not to notice how many of her personal items were in the room; a shawl lay on the bed, a comb on the counter.

He heard her moving about, then silence. He imagined her taking a deep breath, gathering her composure and preparing to face him.

He stopped pacing when she finally stepped around the screen; all trace of fear was gone. Had it been because he touched her? He frowned at that, then his brow smoothed as he remembered kissing her. There had been no problem there, which was good because he had enjoyed touching her the little he had.

The best approach would be to act as if nothing had happened, which, in truth, nothing had, That might be the only way she would confide in him. There was something in him that desperately wanted her to trust him. He sensed that she was drawn to him, and while he had traded on that type of attraction in the past, he wasn't sure he would be able to do so now, or if he wanted to.

She had called him an honest man, and while his own sense of integrity would never permit him to act without honor, the thought that he could not be truthful with her rankled.

"Are you going back to your uncle's tonight?" Simon looked anywhere but at her. Originally, he had thought she used the room to change from her male attire, but now he thought differently. He had the sneaking suspicion that she would be able to get away from anywhere. It wasn't a particularly comfortable feeling.

"Of course."

She bit her lower lip, and he wished that he didn't notice that it was already full enough to send thoughts of kissing straight to his brain.

"He will expect me."

"Does he know about these little nightly escapades?"

"They're not nightly," she snapped. "He knows that I go to see Ma sometimes," she said in a quieter tone.

Simon would bet a dollar that he had no idea just how his niece visited her sister. He waited until she was ready, then held the door open for her, allowing her to exit.

"You can go on now," she said after locking the door. "I think you have all the answers you came for."

Simon bit the inside of his cheek to keep from laughing. Did she really think that? He hadn't even started. "I insist on walking you part of the way," he said. Even saying so, he looked about to see if there were any buggies heading in the general direction. That was one thing he definitely missed about big cities—their hackney cabs in situations such as this.

Of course, he would follow her all the way home, but she wouldn't know that. Once he saw that she was behind the door and the lamp in what had to be the parlor came on, he turned and headed back to his hotel. He really was going to have to meet with Luke. That was two things he had to discuss with his partner. He wondered if the other man knew how diverting being at the hotel could be.

Simon stopped by the mercantile, slipped around the back and inside. Luke had a gun leveled at him. "Oh, come on, Simon. Can't you just knock?" He lowered the gun and placed in on the table.

"Can't you ever say 'hello?'"

Luke grinned at him and waved him to one of the chairs as he took two glasses from the cabinet and a bottle of whiskey. Pouring them each a healthy measure, he brought them to the table and gave one to his partner. "To what do I owe the pleasure?"

Simon took a long draw of the whiskey. "Did you know that Maj and Kirsten are sisters?"

"No." Luke took a smaller drink from his own glass. "Do you think it matters?"

"I'm not sure. I would say not, but it depends on what Maj has told you. She has told you something of her uncle, hasn't she?"

"Not much. Her mother's brother and he took them from Minnesota where they had been quite happy." He shrugged. "That was about it. Did Kirsten say something different?"

"Not at all. Much the same." He wasn't ready to tell Luke that he suspected said uncle also beat Kirsten. She wouldn't admit it yet, and he had no way of knowing if Maj received the same treatment. There was no sense in raising his friend's ire for no reason. He was plenty riled up for the both of them. He took another sip of his drink and reminded himself that he had to be objective or he would learn nothing.

"I think it's time we find out what Weldon is up to."

"I thought that's what we *were* doing?"

Simon tossed back the rest of his drink and placed the glass on the table with a satisfying *thunk*. "I don't seem to be any closer to the truth now than I was a few days ago. Besides, I wonder if someone doesn't suspect us—well, me."

Luke raised his eyebrows in question.

So Simon told him about the incident in the hotel. "Take it as a warning to be on guard." As if the man needed it. He never met anyone better at seeing trouble around any corner unless it was himself.

"Interesting. I did say things tend to happen when you're around, Simon."

He inclined his head in agreement. "And then tonight, I

go to my room to find Kirsten waiting for me."

"Go on." But there was a smile playing about Luke's lips.

Simon chuckled at him. "Not what you're thinking, I assure you. She wanted me to get her on a train out of here. I found it very interesting when later she met Maj. That was before I learned she had a sister."

"So, what is your plan now?"

"I'm going to Weldon's. You find out from Maj about Kirsten, what she was planning."

"You don't need help at Weldon's?"

"I hope not. But if you don't see me by dinner tomorrow, you'll know where I am."

Rising, he headed for the door and walked back to the hotel. Listening carefully, he could detect no one following him, always a good sign. It was an even better sign when he found his room empty.

The next morning, Simon took extra care in dressing in what he considered his best railroad manager suit. Only the best of anything would impress a man of Weldon's stature.

Simon definitely had his number; he had met more than his fair share of the type in his years of service, both in the war and when directly in President Grant's employ.

"What brings you here today?" Weldon greeted him jovially enough.

"Oh, when we were talking earlier, I wanted to make sure I had the figures correct."

A look of irritation crossed Weldon's face, but it was quickly gone. "Told you to write those numbers down."

"So you did." Simon shifted in his saddle, waiting for Weldon to invite him in.

"I have some time this morning, so why don't you come down?" He waved Simon off his horse.

"Sounds good," he said as he dismounted. He tied his horse's reins to the hitching post near the bottom of the porch steps.

"I don't see any paper today either." Weldon tried to sound amused, but to Simon it just sounded irritated. That was fine with him.

He patted his jacket pocket. "Right here."

Weldon motioned him in. "We may as well go into the office today. It'll be easier to just show you on the map than to ride all over the ranch."

"Amen to that," Simon said, and meant it. The exercise didn't bother him, but he had not come up with another way to get into the man's office. "I still feel a bit bruised from the last ride."

Weldon quaffed at that. "Don't imagine you city boys have to spend much time in the saddle."

"That we don't," Simon agreed. No need for the man to know that it wasn't unusual for Simon to spend six or eight hours, or in some cases, even the whole day, in the saddle. That would hardly suit his purpose.

Simon looked over the map where Weldon pointed to different areas, careful to write down the number of cattle the man quoted to him. He noticed that Weldon avoided one area of the map entirely. A map that did not match up with the one Simon had from his Washington office. "What's over here?" he asked, using his pencil to point to one corner of the map.

Weldon looked at the section as if he had never seen it before. "That's pretty undeveloped. We hope to move some cattle out there eventually."

"Looks like it would be a great link up with the railroad," Simon said idly, using his finger to trace the marked path.

The man chuckled, but looked flustered. "No, that's no good." He walked toward his desk.

It was a deliberate ploy to have Simon's gaze follow him and leave the map. Simon went along with it. Weldon reached over for the cigar box and offered one to Simon.

"Seems like it would be an ideal set up," Simon continued after trimming and lighting the cigar.

"It would be," Weldon agreed, "except that it's mostly scrub there. No place for the cattle to rest, you know."

Simon blew smoke from the cigar and leaned back in the chair across the desk from the man, pretending not to know that there was no need for the cattle to rest on the short drive from the pasture to the rail. "Seems a shame. Looks fairly close to the rail line." He watched Weldon with calculated attention, careful to look interested only in his next puff of cigar.

Weldon cleared his throat.

Simon looked up, then got to his feet. "Sorry for taking up your time, Mr. Weldon. I know how busy you are." He patted the pocket with his paper, "But I appreciate you giving me the right numbers."

Weldon slowly got to his feet. "As to that..."

Simon raised his eyebrows in question. "Sir?"

Weldon came around the desk and leaned against it. He took his cigar from his mouth and looked at it while speaking.

"You seem an intelligent man, Mr. Barr."

"Sir?"

"Able to pick out that track as quickly as you did took some skill."

Simon chuckled. "Not really. I do check out everywhere the rail lines go." Not to mention the years of mapping and reading and scouting he had done for the Union. He hadn't been known as one of the top intelligence officers without reason.

"How would you like to do some work for me?"

"I like working for the railroad, Mr. Weldon." He kept his tone of voice respectful and vague. He certainly didn't want the man to think this was a chance too good for him to miss.

Weldon chuckled and looked at him. "Don't disappoint me, Mr. Barr. I want to know if you're interested in working on the side."

Simon took a puff of his cigar. "What did you have in mind?"

"I do have occasion to move other cargo, but I would prefer not to have it widely known. As you so noted, my property is close to that section of the rail. Arrange for another stop there, just for my cargo, and another stop for someone to pick it up and you could make yourself a tidy bundle.

That hit the mark! "I'm not sure I could do that."

Weldon chuckled. "I'm talking about a ten minute delay on either end, if that, and not on every run. I could even arrange to have the pick up at a regular stop so that would not be a problem."

"If you don't mind my asking, sir, why don't you just ship it from the Pine Grove station?"

If Simon hadn't been looking for it, he would have missed the flash of irritation that crossed Weldon's face. He studied his cigar a moment before speaking, careful to only look at Simon in the end.

"Let's say I would be a lot happier if some other people

didn't know what I was shipping. Too many competitors out there, you might say."

Simon nodded. "How much are we talking?"

Weldon chuckled and clamped the cigar back in his mouth for another puff, studying Simon. "Said you were a smart man."

He named an amount that made Simon's eyebrows raise on their own. That was some incentive even for a well paid manager to look the other way for ten minutes. Simon gave a low whistle. "That is certainly something to think about."

"Then you will think about it?"

"I'd like to sleep on it." He watched Weldon reach his hand down to rest on his revolver in his holster, but pretended to not see it.

"As I said, Mr. Barr, you appear to be an intelligent man." Now he blatantly rested his hand on his gun butt and Simon's eyes followed. "I would prefer an answer now."

"I understand that." Simon took a puff of his cigar, pretending to consider the matter. Then he smiled, and extended his hand. "But of course I would be delighted to work with you, Mr. Weldon."

The other man practically heaved a sigh of relief.

"When would you like me to arrange the stops?"

"I'll have a shipment ready in another day or so. I'll send you word at the hotel the night before the delivery. Will that be enough time?"

Simon gave a curt nod. "I do have to wire the offices and give them some type of warning, you understand."

"Of course, of course. Just remember who you're working for."

Simon extinguished his cigar in the ashtray on the desk. "Always, sir, always." Picking up his hat, he followed Weldon to the door and gave him a quick salute on his way out.

Things were definitely looking up, he thought as he rode back to town.

Chapter Five

As soon as he entered town, Simon made his way to the mercantile. He had to send a telegram from somewhere, and that seemed as good a place as any and better than some.

The store was mercifully empty for the moment. "Where is everyone?"

"Hey, it's late in the day. How did it go?"

Simon gave Luke a slow smile. "Just fine. He bit like a hungry fish." He clapped his hands together. "I really need to send a telegram, but it would be best if there were more people about. When is a good time?"

"Time for what, Mr. Barr?" The old biddy, Isabelle, he thought, from the other day, entered the store, her basket over her arm.

"Just talking to my friend here. I need to send a telegram back to the office to let them know how long I'll be about."

"And how long will that be?"

"A few more days, certainly."

She came to stand next to him, resting her basket on the counter and handing Luke a list. "These are the things that I need," she told him, then turned her attention back to Simon. He tried not to let his lips twitch. It didn't help when he heard Luke in his best shopkeeper voice agree to get the things right away.

"I saw you talking to that Maj woman," she said in a rather loud whisper. "At the dance, you know."

Simon turned to lean against the counter, crossing his

arms over his chest. "Yes, I did know. I was talking to her, you understand."

Isabelle sniffed the air. "I can't imagine what she was even doing there. That's not a place for a woman like her."

"Like her? I'm afraid I don't understand. She seemed quite pleasant to me."

"Of course you would say that. You're a man!"

Simon inclined his head. "Nice of you to notice." He ignored Luke's cough from somewhere behind him.

Biddy—Isabelle—leaned closer to him. "She's not a decent sort, you know. She should stay where she belongs."

"And just where might that be?" He kept his voice neutral. Even if he hadn't known that she was Kirsten's sister, he knew that she was much kinder than this woman in front of him.

"With...with those other loose women. Dances are for the nice, genteel women to meet eligible men."

"Really? I thought they were a place for people to gather and enjoy the music and themselves."

She shook her head. "I do wonder about you, Mr. Barr. I thought someone from the city would have more sense."

"Here you are, ma'am," Luke said, placing the order on the counter, the items making a satisfying thump as they connected with the surface.

Simon could see the sparks practically flying from the man's eyes, but Luke kept his face bland while he tallied the bill and made change for the woman. As he was handing it to her, two other women came in. One Isabelle's age and one much, much younger.

"How do you do, Isabelle?" The older woman said, coming to where they were standing.

Simon turned to Luke. "I think I'd like to send that telegram, please."

"Certainly." Luke passed him a piece of paper and he quickly wrote several words on it. Seeing what they were, Luke was careful to sound it all out before accepting payment. Here for a few more days was all the women wanted to hear.

As he finished, Simon turned to leave, only to find himself hemmed in by the newcomer and who he supposed was her daughter.

He found he was correct when the woman introduced

him. "We are so delighted to have new people visit our town, Mr. Barr. You will join us for dinner tonight, won't you?"

"I'd love to, but I already have plans," he told them.

"Surely you can rearrange them. Miranda here will be so disappointed if you don't join us, won't you, dear?"

The young woman's blonde curls danced as she nodded. "Oh, yes. I would just love to hear all about the big cities. Mama said that you come from New York. I bet it's wonderful there, all the latest fashions..."

"Yes, quite," her mother interrupted her. "Do say you'll come."

"I'm afraid I really must refuse," Simon insisted pleasantly. "Another time, perhaps. I know that since Luke is here, I will be returning."

"But you already said that you would be staying several more days."

"So I did. Unfortunately, it will be for business reasons, I assure you."

Turning her back on him, the woman quickly made her purchases and left, towing her daughter after her.

Luke came around the side of the counter and leaned against it, joining Simon. "It's that kind of attitude toward Maj that makes me angry."

"Speaking of..."

"Sime, it's not even noon. When was I going to talk to her? Some of us are honest, hard working people who have a store to run."

Simon straightened, and chuckled. "So it seems. Join me for dinner?"

Nodding agreement, Luke watched Simon leave the store.

Simon headed to the Weldon Bank & Trust. It had been several days, time to see if anything had changed in that amount of time. Making sure to visit a different teller, he withdrew a larger amount than he had on his previous visit.

Again, the bills looked genuine. He slipped them into his billfold, and headed for his hotel, thankful to reach his room without being accosted. Although he did wonder about Kirsten; he hadn't seen her yet today, but he was certain that he could find out about her if he had to. He scowled because it was becoming quite clear to him that he would have to. For his own peace of mind.

He took the opportunity to rest for a bit when he was in his room. He had a feeling this was going to be another long night. They seemed to be adding up rather quickly lately.

Meeting Luke in the dining room later, they headed for their table and ordered.

"Any word?" That was not what he had planned to ask, yet it was the first thing out of his mouth.

"Maj didn't come in today," he said. "That's rather unusual."

Simon waved it away. "Let's enjoy dinner and work afterwards. Besides, I may be paying Maj a visit myself, this evening."

Luke stared at him, anger bristling.

"Calm down. I have questions."

"You can ask her during the day."

"Can I? You already saw the old biddy. Don't you trust me?"

Luke scowled at him. "I trust you."

Simon hid his grin. He knew Luke did trust him, but it didn't hurt to tweak his tail a bit. "We have work later."

"Thought you were going to visit Maj."

"What? You can't come with me?"

After dinner, Luke followed Simon to his room. "So, what do you have?"

Simon tossed his billfold on the dresser. "New bills, and an offer." He quickly outlined his visit with Weldon.

"Which is what the telegram was about this afternoon," Luke said. He reached over and picked up Simon's billfold, withdrawing several of the crisp bills. "Brand new."

"Exactly. I don't think they came from the Treasury, but I haven't had time to examine them."

Luke brought the bills to the table and turned up the wick on the oil lamp, then pulled a loupe from the recesses of his coat pocket.

Coming to see what his partner was doing, he said, "That's what I love about you, Luke. Always prepared."

He grunted in response, not looking up from his task. "Hey, Sime, do you have another bill? One that we know *did* come from the Treasury?"

"One minute." Reaching into the pocket inside his coat, he withdrew a small match flint box, which he flipped over, and removed the back.

"Talk about being prepared," Luke said wryly, accepting the twenty-dollar bill.

Simon closed the back and slipped it back in his pocket. "Never know when you might need it.

Luke snorted, then bent to his task again. "Give me another new bill," he told Simon, not looking up from his comparison.

Simon slipped it to him, laying it on the other side of the authentic Treasury bill.

Finally, Luke straightened. "That, without a doubt, is the very best I have ever seen."

"So they are forgeries?"

"Most definitely. But I tell you, Simon, they are going to be deuced difficult to tell, especially if they get mixed in with the real bills."

"You know what this will do to the economy if that happens," Simon said.

"If I didn't, and if the President didn't, I don't think we would be here right now," he said wryly.

"True." Simon leaned over the table and stared at the bills. "So, what am I looking for?"

Luke ran his hand through hair, then motioned Simon to pull up a chair. "I need to find another loupe," he said, "but, for now, we can share."

Simon accepted it from him. "So it's not visible to the naked eye?"

"It might be once you know what to look for, but in case there's any doubt, the least you'll need is the loupe."

Nodding, Simon placed it in his eye and reached for the real bill and the counterfeit. Using his finger, Luke traced the differences, pointing them out. They were minor indeed.

Simon removed the loupe and placed it on the table. "That is incredible."

"I'm telling you, they are the best I've ever seen. But now that we've seen them, how are we going to detect them easily?"

Leaning back in his chair, Simon tapped his finger against his lips. "If we think that Weldon is still behind this..."

Luke snorted as he pulled out the other chair and turned it, straddling it and resting his arms on the back. "Have you seen anything that would suggest he's not in on it? From what you've said, and what's in the dossier, there can be no doubt."

"I'm thinking there isn't. The man was willing to shoot me rather than let me walk out of that office without agreeing to his terms."

"I would expect no less. So, should we accept that the first shipment will be counterfeit bills?"

"I think I'm going to have to wait until tomorrow evening, at the earliest, to find out. In the meantime, I think we need to see who else is working with Weldon. I don't see this as a one man show. I have been all over his spread and haven't seen anything that would indicate there was a counterfeit operation."

"I hardly think they're going to point it out to you!"

Simon gave him a wry smile and shook his head. "Luke, Luke. Do give me some credit. There were no stacks of goods that were not accounted for."

"So, they have to be mixed in with what is accounted for, right? Elementary."

Simon waved it away. That was elementary. "Well. That's as far as we can take it tonight. Do you want to wire Washington?"

Luke stood. "Absolutely delighted to do so." He watched as Simon stood, too, and reached for his hat. "And what do you plan on doing this evening?"

"Think I'll head to the saloon and see what I can find there. Were you planning to join me?" He didn't remind his partner that he was thinking of trying to see either of the women. He wasn't sure what he would say if he caught either one.

"Not tonight." He picked up both bills and held them out to Simon. "I plan to take these back and see if there is some easy, tell-tale method we can use to determine which is authentic." He folded the bills and slipped them in his jacket pocket. "I'll see you tomorrow," he said, slipping out the door.

Simon was right behind him, closing and locking the door after him.

ӟ ӟ ӟ

Kirsten blew at the tendrils of hair that had escaped her bun as she bent over her work. Her uncle had wanted yet another story on Weldon. It was bad enough when she had to write the others, but this one she had to typeset since the man usually responsible for the task was out of town—at her uncle's request.

She had been mortified when Simon—Mr. Barr—had seen her back. How could she explain that it was her own stupidity that led to receiving the lashes? The other scars were not so noticeable now and she was sure he wouldn't have been at all aware of them if it hadn't been for the new ones.

She smiled wryly. Not that he should have seen them anyway. No gentleman would have come behind that screen. Not that he ever claimed to be a gentleman, but she had thought of him as such.

She heard her uncle's footsteps near the door, so she hurriedly bent to her task, sliding more type into the slot.

"Ain't you done with that yet?"

"Nearly so." She straightened and looked down at the work. She still had about ten lines on the story before she finished. The regular typesetter was much, much quicker at it, but there wasn't much she could do about that.

Her uncle came near her and leaned over the tray where she was setting the type. He gave a loud grunt.

She slid out the next tray and quickly picked out the letters she would need. "I told you it would have been better if I had gone on the errand and Samuel finished the typesetting."

"It needed a man to do the job," he said. "Besides, no matter what I think about you, you're my niece and you have ink in your blood. But you've taken so long that dinner is well over. And don't think you'll be looking for something, 'cause nothing was left. There was a guest joining us tonight." He turned on his heel after delivering his message and closed the door after him. She half expected to hear the lock turn, but there was silence. At least until her stomach growled. She knew she should be used to it, but she wasn't. She had eaten the apple she had in her room much earlier. She was almost hungry enough to contemplate eating the stale bread she had hidden in her drawer.

Walking to her desk, she opened the top drawer and pulled out the napkin. The bread was still there and looked no more appetizing than it had earlier. It hadn't been all that fresh to begin with. She wrapped it back up and shoved it in the drawer. She would see if Maj had anything saved for her. Sometimes she did. If not, the bread couldn't get too much worse in the next hour or so. She wrinkled her nose at the thought.

She had learned not to be too fastidious while living with her uncle, and things that she thought she would never eat, she ate without too much complaint, but there were times it became a bit overwhelming. She thought back to the dinner she had shared with Simon. He had no way of knowing how much she had appreciated it, probably viewing her thanks as mere politeness.

Ignoring the protests of her stomach for the time being, she quickly finished her task and marked that the article was finished. She had to play around with the words in the end in order to get everything to fit, but finally, she was done. Stripping off the black cuffs she used to keep the ink from her sleeves, she laid them on the bench, and then went to clean her hands.

Picking up her cloak and slipping it over her shoulders, she headed down the back stairs only to stop a few steps from the bottom. She could clearly hear her uncle talking in the shop room, and from the tone of voice he used, she strongly suspected he was speaking to Greg Weldon. His words confirmed it.

"You need to bring Maj back here," Weldon said. "I can't have my future wife's sister being gossiped about."

"She's making decent money where she is," her uncle said. "And a man's gotta have some comfort."

Weldon scoffed. "You have enough money now, and you know you'll have more shortly. Even sooner than we expected." There was a clink of glass on glass, then silence for a moment before he continued. "I talked to that railroad manager today. Understanding man, there."

Her uncle chuckled. "So he agreed to your terms?"

"I didn't exactly leave him much choice," he said dryly. "The good thing is that he had to come back because he forgot to write stuff down. I can see that he'll have limited usefulness."

Simon! They were talking about Simon. She sank against the wall. Had Simon known Weldon all along? She hurried down the stairs and exited the door before her uncle could stop her—if he had even heard her.

All the way to Maj's she wondered what the men had been talking about. But the fact that Weldon wanted to move the wedding up disturbed her more than anything. That had to be what he had been referring to in saying that her uncle would soon have even more money. She knew she would have to do something drastic, would have to leave. She would definitely have to warn Maj. Perhaps she could get her sister to live behind Doc's. Very few people knew of the room's existence. In fact, she wondered that she had not thought of it before when the women in town started gossiping about Maj and what her true role was at Kate's.

The place really wasn't large enough to live in and, if anyone found out, it would give rise to other gossip. She wasn't that naïve.

Slipping down the alleyway, she made her way to Kate's and beneath Maj's window and scooped up a few stones. She was ready to throw one when she heard a footstep on the gravel, and then *his* voice.

"You don't have to do that, you know. I'm sure Kate would let you in the door, or the cook would from the back."

She turned to face him. "What are you doing here?" she hissed. She wanted to be irritated, but she couldn't stop the leap of joy she felt.

"Waiting for you."

How she wished he were, but not the way he meant it. She lowered her arm when she realized that she was foolishly still holding the stones, and let them slide from her hand. "How did you know I would be here?"

"I didn't. I hoped." He pushed himself away from the post he was leaning against.

"What do you want?" She tried to keep the suspicion out other voice, but knew it was there. She *was* suspicious, after all. What could he want with her?

Simon held out his hands, palms up. "Why, to see you, what else? You won't tell me where you live, so I have to meet you where I can." Using his chin, he pointed to her gown. "You're not planning to play cards tonight, I take it."

"No. No, I'm not. I just left the newspaper."

"And came to pay a nightly visit to your sister."

"It's not nightly," she said, though why she felt she had to justify herself, she didn't know. Besides, Weldon said Simon worked for him now. Did that mean he was waiting for

Maj too. She asked him.

If he was feigning surprise, it was the best she had seen. "Why would I do that?"

"You tell me, Mr. Barr, Weldon said—" She immediately clamped her hand over her mouth. She had not meant to say that. There was no sense in hoping that he hadn't caught it. His eyes narrowed as he studied her.

He reached out a hand and grasped her arm. "I think we need to talk."

She pulled away, but he hauled her closer, close enough that he could whisper in her ear. "We can do this easily, or not, but we will talk. Now, I suggest you come with me. We're going to slowly walk to the mercantile."

When she nodded that she understood, he gentled his hold on her arm, but she was quite aware of the leashed strength of him, and knew if she tried to move too far, he would have no qualms in pulling her back to his side.

He didn't say anything on the short walk, but she was aware of his tension. Fortunately, there were very few people about. When the sheriff came down the street, she considered calling out to him, but Simon's voice rumbled in her ear as if he had known her very thought. "Don't even consider it." He nodded to the sheriff and continued.

Once at the store, he went around the back. She wondered if she should be frightened, but didn't have time to consider it. Reaching out one fist, he thumped on the door and it was opened immediately by Luke. "Nice of you to knock," he wryly greeted Simon. "What brings you here?"

Simon pushed Kirsten toward a kitchen chair. He could have been a little gentler; she scowled at him, but doubted that he noticed. He seemed to be concentrating on Luke.

"I think I need some answers, and I have a feeling Miss Kirsten can help me."

"Why should I?" She intended to sound firm, but was afraid it sounded more petulant, especially when Simon just gave her his slow smile in response. She blinked once, trying to refocus her thoughts. She wished he wouldn't do that.

Luke cleared his throat. "Coffee?"

Simon gave a brief nod. Before Kirsten could answer, her stomach gave an embarrassingly loud rumble.

"I take it that's a yes," Luke said as he set about gathering mugs and reaching for the pot on the stove.

Kirsten nodded without looking at him. "Please."

Once Luke served the coffee, he joined them at the table. "So, why are we all here?"

"I'd like to know that myself," Kirsten said. Sensing that Luke was an ally, she turned to face him. "I was just visiting my sister, or trying to, when Mr. Barr came by and said we have to talk and here we are." She spread her hands wide before letting them rest on the table.

Luke chuckled, but sent a questioning glance Simon's way. "I can believe that. Simon does have a way with women."

She tried not to wince. She deserved that. She took another sip of her coffee and hoped they would blame her flushed cheeks on the heat from the coffee and not from embarrassment. What had made her think that someone like Simon was interested in her personally? Of course, now that she knew he worked for that snake, Weldon, she doubted that she would really be interested in him. She placed her cup on the table, embarrassed again to see that she had drained more than half of it and the men hadn't even touched theirs.

Simon turned his bright blue gaze on her. "Are you hungry?"

She wasn't sure how to answer, but then her stomach rumbled again. She gave him a tight smile. "It seems I could say one thing and my stomach another! But I'm fine."

Simon scowled at her, then stood and started to rummage around in Luke's cupboards and icebox. Finally, he placed a few slices of ham and some beans on a plate in front of her.

She looked at him warily, wondering what she was going to have to answer for her meal. Luke must have interpreted her look correctly because he just smiled at her when he handed her the silverware and encouraged her to eat. "Don't worry about him," he said, cocking his head toward Simon.

Easy for him to say. He hadn't been dragged over here, nor was he getting dagger-like looks sent in his direction.

As if sensing he was the source of her discomfort, Simon continued to stand and paced the room, periodically looking out of the window.

"Will you sit down?" Luke finally said.

"I can't," Simon said simply. "Something is not quite right

and I can't put my finger on it." He paced again, then stopped suddenly as if remembering something. "Did you send that telegram earlier?" he asked Luke.

"Yes, and got a response."

Kirsten expected to hear more, or have him turn over that response, but there was nothing. She cut another piece of ham and chewed slowly. This was wonderful, and she said so.

When she finished, she laid her silverware on the plate, and Simon was immediately next to her, arms braced against the table and looking down at her. "Why did you want to see your sister tonight?"

"Oh, come on, Sime! They're sisters." Luke sounded exasperated.

Simon just waited for her to answer. She could at least give him part of it. "I was hungry," she said. Neither man seemed to dispute that.

"Does she always feed you?" Simon barked.

At least he straightened and she could take a breath without inhaling his. Kirsten shifted in her chair to look at Simon. "Oh, no. Nothing like that. It was just one of those nights when I was working late and I know that sometimes Maj keeps something in her room." Just in case Kirsten stopped by, but she didn't say that part.

Simon rested his chin on his hand, and his elbow on the table, staring at her. "That's it?" He gave her a slow smile. "And here I was thinking it was something urgent."

She bit her lip in indecision. "Not urgent, exactly, but I thought there was something she should know."

Chapter Six

"Know what?" Simon couldn't resist. He laid his hand on the top of her head, enjoying the feel of her silky hair under his callused palm. "You can tell us, Kirsten." He let his hand slide down the back of her head before releasing her. He sensed Luke's sharpened gaze, but wouldn't look in his direction. He crossed his arms, waiting for her to speak.

He knew Luke was on pins and needles waiting to hear what Kirsten had to say, as he was, even if it was for a different reason. Luke was worried about Maj. Simon just needed information on the case. That was it. All that it could be. He ignored the tug on his heart when Kirsten seemed to fight with the decision to speak to them.

Finally, she pushed the chair from the table and stood, turning her back to them.

Simon let her go.

"Mr. Weldon visited my uncle tonight."

Simon tamped down his excitement; she knew something. The plot thickened. It also served as the perfect reminder why Kirsten could and should not matter to him. She was probably involved in this case up to her pretty little neck no matter how much he wished she wasn't. He hoped, for Luke's sake, that the same was not true for her sister.

"What exactly is it that your uncle does, Kirsten?" Luke's voice sounded calm. Enough so that Kirsten seemed to have no problem answering it.

"He's a printer. He runs the weekly paper and the town

news sheet when the mayor decides to run one, and any time the sheriff needs some posters, he does them."

Simon shot a warning look to Luke, stopping him from saying anything more. Simon had a difficult time banking his own anticipation. If Weldon was visiting her uncle... The possibilities were tremendous.

"Why does Weldon need something printed?" Is that how they were partners and it really had nothing to do with the ranch? He hadn't considered that possibility, but it was impossible to dismiss the connection between a printer and a suspected counterfeiter.

She turned to face them, and waved away the question. "He doesn't. He was there to see my uncle about the wedding. I'm supposed to marry him, you know." She gave them a wry smile. "He really wanted to marry Maj first. Now I think he wishes to again."

"But you're the one engaged to him," Simon pointed out.

"Yes." She heaved a sigh, but wouldn't look at him. "He wants to move the date forward."

Simon glanced at Luke. Aside from the slight flaring of his nostrils, he made no reaction.

Kirsten nodded. "Maj didn't want to marry him—doesn't want to—but she can't afford to leave the area too soon because she won't have enough money to live on, or even to get to her destination."

"Which is?"

Kirsten gave Simon a tired smile. "You don't think I'm going to tell you that, do you? It doesn't matter much now since I'm the one who is engaged to him. Besides, I've already said too much since you already work for the man."

"I do?" Simon blinked in surprise.

"That's what he told my uncle."

"I see." Before he could say more, Luke interrupted with his own questions.

"You know, I've never completely understood just why Maj works at Kate's—as a housekeeper," he hastily tacked on when she started to protest.

So, she told him.

"Is that why you offered Weldon money at the card game? To buy him off so he wouldn't be interested in marrying either of you?"

Her eyes widened in surprise.

"Yes, Simon told me."

She shot a reproachful glance in his direction, but he just held her gaze steadily. "Luke and I don't have any secrets," he told her flatly. They couldn't afford to. There were times their lives depended on the other being aware of a situation and being able to act in the correct manner.

"What else did Weldon have to say?" Luke continued.

She turned her head to look at him again. "He doesn't want her working at Kate's. It's one of the reasons he decided to marry me."

Luke snorted. "I didn't think the man and I had anything in common." He pushed himself away from the table and snapped his fingers. "This could be absolutely perfect," he told Simon before addressing Kirsten. "You tell your sister that I can use some help here, at the mercantile."

Kirsten's face brightened, then fell. "I appreciate it, Mr. Hayden, but we have to see if Uncle Ralph will let her come back to his house. Maj is not that strong, and it might not be good for her."

Luke looked puzzled, but Simon cleared his throat, getting his partner's attention. He gave a nearly imperceptible shake of his head that Luke interpreted correctly, and ceased asking questions. Simon had a sneaking suspicion that the strength Kirsten mentioned had to do with the whip marks on her back. His muscles tightened and he had to force himself to relax. He could not wait to get his hands on this uncle, and the reasons why he should just kept growing. As soon as possible, he was going to see what he could find out about the man; he would go to Washington himself and get the information if he had to.

"It's getting late," Simon said. "How about if I walk you back, Kirsten? All the way home this time?"

Thanking Luke for the meal, she gathered her cloak and followed Simon out the door before answering. "I don't know that will be a good idea, Mr. Barr."

Simon reached out and took her hand, tucking it under his arm. "I absolutely insist!"

She stiffened, but didn't pull away. Simon counted that as good fortune. Her uncle didn't live far from Doc's. From the street, he could see that there were one or two lamps lit in the one room. Presumably, her uncle was still awake; it wasn't all that late.

When they got to the door, she tried to disengage, but he held her firm. "I insist," he said.

"I have a key," she told him, and this time, he let her hand go, but stood close enough behind her that she could not enter the house without going through him.

Once she retrieved the key from her reticule, he plucked it from her hand. She looked at him with suspicion, but he merely unlocked the door and handed it back to her. Wasn't she used to gentlemen?

"About time you got here, missy," her uncle's voice floated from the other room.

Simon let her walk ahead of him into the room as he looked about the small hall.

"I don't need you much longer," he said by way of a greeting.

His voice sounded much closer now, although Simon hadn't anticipated him walking to the door. Simon remained in the shadow of the doorway. She didn't look back at him; in fact, he wondered if she remembered he was there. Not a very flattering thought. Not when he was aware of her every breath.

"Where were you? Out cavorting with some of them cow-hands, I bet. You listen here." He took another step closer, and reached his hand out to drag her toward him.

He stopped in surprise when his own arm was grasped in a crushing vise.

Simon stepped from the shadows, and guided the older man further into the room, closer to the light. "I think you should apologize to the lady," he said in a low voice.

"Now, look here, I don't rightly know who you are—"

"Simon Barr. Definitely not a cowhand."

"Ah, yes, the big city railroad manager that Weldon has working for him."

Simon ignored that. It didn't matter what the man said as long as Simon got what he wanted. Right now, what he wanted was to rub this man's face on the ground, but that wasn't to be just yet. He pulled the man's arm up tighter. "I said you should apologize."

"What for? That's my niece. Ain't nothing to you." The man looked him up and down with suspicion in his eyes. "Or is she your fancy-piece? You better think of sending some of that money this way."

Simon had killed men for less. He heard Kirsten give a mewling sound and was gone. He didn't feel far from retching himself, and he had a strong stomach. Instead, he let his right fist connect with the man's midsection until he doubled over. With a sense of dissatisfaction, Simon knew the one blow was going to have to suffice for the moment. He was going to have to keep the man in one piece if he wanted some answers.

Leaving her uncle to catch his breath as he doubled over and sank to the floor, Simon turned on his heel and called for Kirsten. She didn't answer, but he could hear her upstairs. Taking them two at a time, he listened until he pinpointed the room she was in. Half expecting the door to be locked, he nonetheless tried the knob and was surprised that it opened readily under his hand.

She was lying across the bed, face down, heaving dry sobs. Not a good sign. His sisters mostly subscribed to the throwing things against the wall theory. When they cried, there was plenty of wailing and liquid tears to accompany them.

"Kirsten?" He called her name softly.

She pulled one arm tighter over her head, but didn't answer.

"Kirsten, listen to me," he repeated. He stooped down beside her and let his hands fall between his legs. He wanted to touch her, but was afraid to at that moment. She seemed brittle. Her uncle had been insulting to him, and more so to her. He wondered how many such insults she had endured, and marveled that she had stayed. That seemed a mystery worth unraveling. "I have to leave," he told her softly. For more reasons than one, even if the most pressing was the damage he feared he would do to the man downstairs.

"I understand."

Her voice was muffled, but at least she had responded. He couldn't resist. He sank to his knees on the floor and reached his hand out to gently rub it across her back. She stiffened at first, but then slowly relaxed. "No, I don't think you do," he said. Tendrils of her hair caught on his lips; he didn't brush them aside. As much as he wanted, he couldn't explain all the reasons he had to leave to her, not even to himself at that point. "Kirsten, it's not safe for you to stay here tonight."

She turned her head then, looking at him from one red-rimmed eye. "I stay here every night. I'll be fine."

Simon didn't say anything at first, but lightly traced where he knew the welts were on her back. "I don't want you to stay here tonight."

She turned her face down on the bed again, heaved a sigh, then scrambled to sit up.

Simon moved to assist her, but she brushed him away. "I'm fine." She ran her hand over her face as he fished his handkerchief out of his coat pocket and handed it to her. She didn't look at him, but accepted it and buried her face in its folds, giving a shuddering sigh.

He stood and cupped her shoulders with his hands, urging her to stand too. When she was in front of him, he pushed the strands of her hair that escaped her knot away from her face. "Stay behind Doc's tonight if you have to," he told her, "but don't stay here."

She nodded in agreement. "Although I have never stayed there overnight."

"I have to do some things, but when I'm done, I will come by."

He felt her stiffen beside him, but before she could make any remark, he placed his finger on her lips. "I'm excellent at guard duty." He smiled reassuringly down at her. She gave a reluctant smile in return.

"Now, pack a few things and I'll be downstairs. I want your uncle to understand you will be leaving."

Bentzer was waiting for him when he went downstairs. With the mood Simon was in, he hoped her uncle would say one wrong thing. If he just looked at him wrong, Simon would have him nailed to the floor and enjoy doing it.

The man was sullen, but made no threatening moves, to Simon's dismay. "She leaves this house, she's never coming back. I don't need gossip about my family."

"Is that a fact? Don't worry, old man, she's not coming back." He would find something for her to do—send her to his family, or at least send to them for suggestions. They would love to help. He wasn't the only one with a sense of adventure; it was just easier because he was male!

"You don't mean that, Uncle?"

Simon whirled to see Kirsten at the bottom of the steps. He couldn't tell if she was upset or relieved at her uncle's words.

Her uncle looked pointedly at her bag. "Oh, I mean it. Bad enough people talk about your sister working at that place."

Kirsten dropped her bag and headed closer her uncle. She stopped just out of arm's reach. "My sister! You're the one who sent her to work there!"

After seeing the interaction between uncle and niece earlier, Simon had wondered how she had stood up to him; now he knew. He worried that he would have to drag her off the man.

The older man literally wrung his hands together. "What else could I do? She can't write like you can, she can't manage to do anything in that print shop right, and I don't need another mouth to feed. Besides, with your sister there, I knew you would stay right where you are, and you have until now. Until this fancy railroad manager came along." He jerked his thumb in Simon's direction, then stepped closer to her.

Simon shifted his weight to the balls of his feet, waiting to see if he had to pull the man back. It would give him great pleasure to do so.

"You're really leaving? Just like that?"

"Just like that," Kirsten said as she stepped around him.

As if realizing that he needed her for something after all, he said, "If you walk out that door, you'll never see your sister again! I'll make sure Weldon knows. He knows enough people that she can just disappear." He snapped his fingers to emphasize his point.

Simon didn't doubt it. Kirsten raised her chin in the air and Simon recognized the defiant gesture for what it was. She didn't know, but he had already planned that neither of the women would be married to Weldon. He intended to get Kirsten out of his sphere and, as for Maj, well, Luke had already expressed his interest. He had no idea what her feelings were on the subject, but he trusted Luke implicitly in everything else; he wasn't going to start doubting him now. If he believed his feelings were reciprocated, Simon would go with that.

Picking up Kirsten's bag, Simon held the door open for her. She left without looking back. The door slammed after them, and Simon breathed a sigh of relief. The walk to Doc's was short indeed from her house. After checking that the little room was free of any visitors, he encouraged her to get into bed.

"I think I'll stay up for a while," she told him.

Simon chuckled softly. "Kirsten, I'll be here."

"You said you have something to do."

He gave a curt nod. "It'll take a bit of time, but I will come back after that. There's no reason for you to not get comfortable."

Her wary look made him reassure her about his guard duty ability, unlikely though it might be for a railroad manager. "I wasn't always a railroad manager. I spent a good amount of time in the Union Army. Does that make you feel better?"

"Perhaps I should come with you."

"I don't think that's necessary."

She gave him a tired smile, but did as he bid and began to straighten up a corner of the room.

He quickly glanced over the room. There was the one bed, not even a bed, he noted, but a cot. One of the girls would have to sleep on the floor.

Simon hoped she would rest easy knowing that he would be keeping watch. It rather surprised him at how much her trust mattered to him. He resisted touching her. "I'll be back as soon as I can."

True to his word, he was back before the half hour was up with Maj in tow. As soon as Maj saw her, she opened her arms and the two girls hugged.

"I can see I'm not needed," Simon interrupted them as he followed Maj in the door and made certain they had what they needed for the night.

Assuring herself that he would soon return, Kirsten watched him leave, then turned to her sister and explained what she had overheard.

"You can't marry him, Kirsten. There's something about him..."

They sat on the edge of the bed, heads bent close together. It was a comfort just to be together. "I'm just glad you're out of that place."

"I might be out, but if we plan to eat, I need to go back. It's not a bad job."

"Maj, Weldon wants you out of there." She chuckled. "Actually, I think everyone wants you out of there except Uncle Ralph."

Her sister raised frightened eyes to her. "He's evil, Kirsten. He scares me."

"Uncle? He can be frightening, but I don't know that he's evil."

Maj shook her head. "Greg. Weldon."

Kirsten gave a tight laugh. "Well, he scares me too. He's not even interested in the money. You know I tried to buy our freedom, and he just didn't care. Told me there wasn't enough money and to go away." Of course, if he had known it was she, he hadn't let on and she saw no reason to enlighten him. There was no sense in mentioning that part to her sister now.

₴ ₴ ₴

Simon ran through the alleyway, to Luke's. This was definitely an unforeseen development. He had meant what he said; he would not have Kirsten return to her uncle's.

"What right do you have to make that decision?" Luke asked him after Simon entered the rooms. Luke wasn't often exasperated, but this appeared to be one of those few and far between times. Simon knew his partner was in the right of it.

Simon ran his hand down his face. "None. That's not the problem here." It only complicated the real problem, and he knew it, especially since Weldon was involved in both. "But, Luke, she can't stay there." He set his jaw on that. "No one should be subject to that kind of treatment." He wasn't going to go into detail, not even with Luke. That really was crossing the line; it was Kirsten's story to tell or withhold. He would reconsider if it would make a difference in the case, but it wouldn't.

"Come on, Sime. No matter how bad it is, it wouldn't be for much longer. You know we're close to solving this."

"Not close enough." He switched the conversation to the real matter at hand. "I have to say, Luke, those bills are worrying me more than I would like."

"You're not the only one. Which reminds me," he said. Turning from where he was standing near the table, he walked over to the small desk tucked against the corner and reached for a paper. "This telegram came through earlier."

"In the store?" Simon asked idly while reaching for the message.

"Back here. It's from the President."

Simon read it quickly. "He's worried about the shipment that's coming to the Treasury Department tomorrow." He handed the paper back to Luke, who took it and tossed it into the small fire burning in the grate.

"But that shipment isn't coming from here."

Simon pushed away from the doorframe where he was leaning and started to pace. "Why would he think they're not Treasury backed bills? He didn't say that."

"No, but think about it. If the shipment of real bills is coming from Denver, it has to come through here. Maybe he thinks there's going to be a switch."

Simon stopped and stared at him. "And he just might be right!" He ran his hand across the back of his neck. "I was so busy thinking about what Weldon would be doing, of how he would be loading his bills, that I didn't even consider that he might actually be *switching* bills."

"If that's the case, then one of us better be on that train."

"And I guess that someone will be you," Simon said. "After all, I'm to be working with Weldon."

"I'll meet up with some of the other agents in town tomorrow afternoon. Major Trent said they would be available," he said, naming the man in charge of their operations.

Simon nodded. "Good move. The Major's last orders before I left were to the effect that we shouldn't do this alone."

Luke shot him a wry grin and put his hands in the air, palm out. "I'm not saying anything."

Simon didn't bother suppressing the chuckle that crossed his lips. He was known for doing things on his own. He didn't always intend it that way. It was just that events often moved too quickly to call for reinforcements, such as Luke was doing now.

Walking over to his desk and pulling the telegraph key toward him, Luke let the Major know they had the situation under control for the time being. Once that was completed, he sent a message to the train station in Pine Grove letting them know they would be picking up a passenger, and additional guards.

"Done?" Simon asked after it appeared all transactions were completed.

At Luke's nod, Simon suggested he come with him for the rest of the night. In this case, four eyes were better than two.

Once at Doc's, Simon gave a soft rap on the door, which was immediately opened.

"I'm glad you're still here," he said. He stepped aside so that she could see Luke was with him.

Maj immediately held out her hand, which Luke clasped as he stepped past Simon, who followed more slowly. The room was quite crowded with the four of them standing about.

"Maj has decided to stay here for the night," Kirsten said. "Tomorrow she will go back, but I will feel safer with some-one here."

"You're safe; your uncle is not coming, you know," Simon said. He looked about; the room was terribly small. Tugging on Maj's hand, Luke led her outside. From the doorway, Simon could see that Luke stood very close to Maj, locking them in their own private space. If the other couple stayed on the threshold, that would give him a little more privacy in questioning Kirsten. He tried not to look at Luke, wishing he was in a similar position, but that would be foolish. Right now, he had no real proof that Kirsten was not involved.

Chapter Seven

Simon leaned against the door after closing it behind him; he rested on his hands, flattened against the door. Luke would stand guard until he came back out. But it was time, way past time, that he learned what hold Kirsten's uncle had over her.

With a small, still thinking part of his brain, he knew that he probably still couldn't take her answer as solid truth, but he wanted to. Desperately.

"Now, what hold does your uncle have over you?"

She shook her head, but didn't answer him.

He heaved a sigh. That really didn't surprise him; he had just hoped she would confide in him.

She sank down onto the chair near the table. She didn't look at him, but she looked defeated.

Walking to the table, he braced his hands against the edge next to her. He didn't want to touch her just yet; he wanted her to feel comfortable enough to talk to him. Right now, he needed information. Any that she could give him. He doubted that anything she could tell him about her relationship with her uncle would have any bearing on his case, but it would allow him to learn more about her. He brushed the thought aside, telling himself that this case was his main purpose for being in the area. He had a sinking feeling she was rapidly becoming his main purpose. Period. That was not necessarily a good thing when he was on the job. He did not need to be distracted, did not want to overlook anything, and right now, she was tied up with Weldon, his number one suspect. But it nagged him that her uncle might fit in. He was a printer. Who better? If both men, both close to her, were involved, how could she not be?

Perhaps she knew and was playing along. He gritted his teeth; he refused to believe it. "Look, Kirsten, if you don't tell me what's going on, I can't help you."

She lifted her gaze to his then. "Help me? Why would you? Not that there is anything for you to help with," she tacked on hastily.

Simon scoffed at that. "Kirsten, I saw the marks on your back. And the man was going to hit you again. There is no reason you should suffer any of that. From anyone, least of all a relative." He had to force himself to stop. Just thinking about it made him tenser. "What hold does he have over you?" This time, he managed to ask in a softer tone of voice.

She bent her head forward, and he could barely hear her, but she was speaking.

Sensing that she was oblivious to him, he left his perch at the table and stooped down beside her, resting on the balls of his feet. He wanted to reach out and touch her, but resisted.

"I...we...owe everything to my uncle," she said.

Her voice dropped lower and he had to lean in to make out her words. He inhaled the scent of her, the one that made him think of lemons and sunshine. This was not good. He started to back away, but she spoke again.

"If it weren't for my father..."

He had to lean closer, but she didn't continue immediately. He could sense Luke's presence as his shadow fell across the window as he paced outside. The last thing he wanted was for them to come in.

Simon could no longer resist and reached out and cupped the back of her neck with his hand, bringing her infinitesimally closer to him. "Tell me, Kirsten." He wanted to promise that it would all be fine, but he had learned a long time ago not to make any rash promises. He had learned to choose his words with care.

"Years ago, after my mother died, my father ran off with Uncle's wife. My Aunt Myra." Again, her voice dropped.

That was definitely not a nice thought, but not horrendous. "Where are they now? Why do you feel you owe your uncle?"

She looked up at him then, and he quickly caught his breath at the sight of her large, green eyes swimming with unshed tears. Inhaling was not good either, he thought, as her scent wrapped itself around his brain.

"They died. Both of them. There was a carriage accident when they were gone for less than a week. In fact, Uncle Ralph wasn't even home when it became known. He was out searching for them."

Simon kept his immediate suspicions to himself. He would love to know just how close the man had been to the accident scene, but knew that was a mean-spirited thought. "So you learned about this on your own?"

"I did have Maj."

Simon shook his head. "How old were you?"

"I was ten and Maj was thirteen. She took care of me."

That rather surprised him. From the little he knew of the sisters' relationship, it seemed that Kristen was the one taking care of matters. It could have been different then, but how much care could a thirteen-year-old give? "And your uncle came for you then?"

She looked startled for a moment, then shook her head and gave him a slow smile, one that went straight to his gut. He cleared his throat and let his hand fall to the back of her chair. Touching her was not a good idea.

"Oh, no. He didn't come for several years."

"How did you survive?" And why had the man finally shown up? Did his conscience get the better of him? Somehow, Simon doubted it; not from what little he knew of the man. One thing for sure, people didn't change who they really, basically were, and he had a feeling that Ralph Bentzer had always been out for himself.

"It wasn't too bad at first," she told him, looking directly at him.

He almost wished she wouldn't do that. He had to force himself to listen to what she was saying and not pay attention to the way her lips formed her words. Now that she had started, she seemed determined to finish.

"The neighbors often came by, made sure we had enough to eat. A couple of them even wanted to take us home with them, but Maj wouldn't let them."

Simon shifted his weight, and in doing so, his arm

brushed Kirsten's shoulders. She opened her eyes wider, but didn't move away, so he left it there, occasionally running his fingers across her back in a soothing motion. The way someone should have done when she was a child.

"That might have been the best thing if you had gone. Little girls need comfort." Visions of his sisters immediately came to mind. They would have been devastated.

"Do you think that's what they offered?" She tilted her head to one side. "I wasn't sure, but Maj thought they would just make us work. Oh, they would have fed us and given us a place to sleep, but Maj took care of me, Mr. Barr. She let me play, let me go to school... I could never do enough to repay her."

"I'm beginning to understand." He was getting a much better picture of what the girls had gone through from her few, well chosen words. He cleared his throat. "What happened after your uncle came?"

Kirsten shrugged. "We went with him, of course. He let us work with him in the newspaper, and he let me finish school. Maj wanted to go back east to college; she wanted to become a teacher, but he said it was too expensive. She wasn't very good at typesetting or being a reporter, so he found another job for her here."

Newspaper. Printing. It all came back to that. The story just got better and better. Or not, he thought, studying her. The last thing he needed was for her to be mixed up in this. And chances were good indeed that she was. He cleared his head, wishing he could give it a good shake. He would puzzle it out later. "But he let you stay with him?"

She nodded, but looked down, not meeting his gaze. He would have preferred looking at her, watching her eyes to see if she really was telling the truth. His gut instinct had never let him down before, but with Kirsten, he was beginning to doubt himself.

"He said that I was quite useful." She looked up at him then and gave him a half smile. "I like to talk a lot, you see, so people would tell me things and I would write them down for the newspaper. I was a news reporter before I was sixteen." Her smile wavered a bit. "My uncle liked that since he didn't have to pay someone else, you see."

Simon stood, letting his hand linger on her shoulder a moment before removing it. He thought he saw quite clearly.

The trouble was that he didn't care for her past as he saw it. It did put her seeming trust in him in perspective. He didn't have to worry that she had singled him out; he probably had just been available. It was a lowering thought.

But what happened now that she was old enough to do something else on her own? Why hadn't she left? He couldn't permit himself to say anything, to promise anything, until he considered the situation a while longer. "Look, you get some rest tonight, you hear?"

She nodded, but made no move to stand.

Simon couldn't resist touching her and ran his hand over her head once more. "Listen, Kirsten, Luke and I will be right outside your door. Your uncle can't get to either of you tonight without going through us. Now, if anything else bothers you during the night, you just let us know."

He left before he did something really stupid. Like kiss her. That would not be in his best interest.

Holding the door open so that Maj could slip inside, Simon closed it after her, leaning against the doorframe.

"Close escape?" Luke asked him dryly.

"You might say that." Simon stood and moved to the side of the porch, indicating Luke should join him. He quickly relayed everything that Kirsten had told him about her uncle.

"Sounds like a bounder, but I don't know that makes him guilty."

"I didn't say he was guilty, but I think he bears watching. Especially taking into consideration the things she said earlier. At the dance," he reminded his partner.

Luke waved that away. "No, I remember what you said. I'm just trying to figure out where Weldon fits into this."

"There must be things about him in the newspaper."

"Exactly! Now I don't mind paying a visit to the newspaper office, but that would leave you here alone."

Simon raised his eyebrow at that. His partner knew that he was well able to handle himself. Then his brow cleared. Perhaps he was concerned because Maj was involved, or even because he noted Simon's interest in Kirsten. "This isn't anything different, Luke."

"Not saying that it is. But if only one of us goes, I think it should be you. Think how satisfying it would be for you to discover what you needed to know about Bentzer."

But what if he found out something about Kirsten, something he wasn't sure he wanted to know? Simon shrugged. Luke knew he liked puzzles, wouldn't be in his line of work, or as successful at it, if he didn't. Still, Simon didn't mind receiving news second hand from a reliable source—meaning Luke or the President.

"I was thinking more along the lines if Bentzer should make an appearance..."

Simon chuckled. "Now that could be satisfying indeed. You let me know if Weldon comes looking for me before then."

Luke touched the brim of his hat in a salute, and leaned against the building. His partner had been brimming with energy. Being held on a tight leash seemed to do that to him. A little physical exercise, in the form of a fistfight, might just be the tonic he needed.

He looked inside the small window. The girls appeared to be sleeping. At least they were in one piece.

* * * *

Kirsten struggled not to toss and turn on her cushioned pallet on the floor. Every time she closed her eyes, the evening's events replayed themselves. She saw Simon's fist connect with her uncle's midsection. The man would never forgive her. Essentially, she was out of a home. She should resent Simon for his high-handedness, but she knew deep down that she did not. If her uncle had turned her out, maybe that would mean that Weldon would no longer be interested in either her or Maj; he could only take so much scandal. That would not be a bad thing.

She glanced at her sister sleeping on the cot. She didn't look any more restful than Kirsten felt.

She allowed herself a small smile. The whole night's work could turn out quite good, actually. If she could get enough money together, she could probably get a job in another town. She was a good newspaper reporter. She and Maj could finally be free. The money she had been giving Maj for use wouldn't be enough for the both of them, but it would be a start.

She fell into a fitful sleep, only to awaken when a large man leaned over her. Too large for Simon. She started to scream, but had a cloth pressed over her mouth. She knew that smell. By the time she placed it, she was losing consciousness. Simon had told her no one would enter but through him, and foolishly she had believed him. She couldn't imagine that she was so valuable that her uncle would kidnap her. On the other hand, why hadn't he just come in himself?

Her last terrifying thought was that the men were not from her uncle at all, but they had made a mistake! She tried to twist her head to see the cot, to see Maj, but it was empty.

* * * *

Simon slid around the side of the newspaper office, careful to stay in the shadows. The building was dark, which he had anticipated. He checked one of the windows, and finding it unlatched, pried it open. Pulling himself up, he was able to slide over the sill and enter the room. He let his eyes adjust to the darkness for a moment, and listened for any unusual sounds indicating that he was not alone.

The front of the office looked much like any other. There was a filing cabinet, but he wasn't ready to search it yet. He was looking for something more recent. The Weldon Bank & Trust was several months old; he doubted if anything written about it would be in the files yet. Slipping into the back room, he looked about. Here, everything was dark. He let his eyes accustom to the inky pitch before he located a lamp, which he lit, keeping the wick low.

Walking the perimeter of the room, alert to any movement or sound, and keeping his back to the wall, he was able to see the large printing press in the center of the room. The type chest sat to one side as did the printer's bench where the plates were made. Those held little interest.

A stack of newsprint caught his attention, and when he went closer to check them out, he gave a satisfied grunt. These were papers from the last two months. He scrambled through the pile, tossing papers aside while hastily reading headlines. There were plenty of write-ups about the new bank opening and all of the benefits it would bring to the town. There wasn't much more. Weldon's name was mentioned a few other times throughout, but most of those were in relation to his cattle ranching. He looked at them more closely. One report did mention that there would be an expansion to the business. Had Kirsten written the story, or had someone else? And was she aware of more than she reported? It would be interesting to find out. For now, his business was done here. He mentally filed the tiny nuggets of information and tidied the pile. Everything was returned to the place he found them, and he exited the way he entered.

Now to share the information, little as it was, and guard duty, with Luke. He scanned the street and the building from several yards away. There was no activity on the street or in front of the building. Nor did Luke appear to be there.

Had the man gone in? Simon knew his partner wouldn't have left. Not without a good reason. Exercising caution, Simon made his way to building, then broke into a low crouched run when he saw Luke lying on the ground. Ascertaining that the man was breathing, Simon pushed open the door, which swung easily under his hand, and peered inside. It was empty. Totally. Both girls were gone. Biting out a curse, Simon hurried back to Luke. He stooped down beside him and shook him. Simon could see a discoloration on the man's jaw, but nothing more.

"Luke!" He hissed his name practically under his breath. "Luke!" He shook him again. This time he was rewarded with a groan.

Luke opened his eyes and stared at Simon, apparently trying to focus. "Sime?" Then, he tried to sit up.

Simon helped him to his feet. "They're gone. What happened?" He guided Luke into the room and closed the door behind them.

"Happened? Damn if I know." He ran his hand over the back of his head. "From the size of the lump on the back of my head I would say someone hit me with a pistol butt."

"From the color of your jaw I thought someone landed a good punch."

"Hmm...I do recall that," Luke said. "Some guy was here. I encouraged him to move along. He swung at me, but that was the last I remember except for the pain to my head." He stumbled to the room and held on to the doorjamb as he looked inside. "Any clues?"

"I didn't look yet. I just got back. Thought I'd check to see if you were alive first," he said dryly.

"Kind of you." Luke's tone matched his friend's. He lit the wick of the lamp on the table, allowing them both to see bet-

ter. Not that there was much. As Simon moved the bed covers, he stopped and sniffed, calling for Luke to do the same.

"Chloroform," Simon said. "That explains why you heard
no struggle. It's also a good indication that, wherever they
are, there's no mistake. They were the ones wanted." He
looked around the room. Something was not right, and he
couldn't pinpoint it. Stooping down, he picked up the cloth
again.

"There's only one," he pointed out to Luke, who shrugged.

"Maybe they only dropped one."

That was the reasonable answer, but Simon *felt* it was
wrong. He scanned the contents of the room again, then
stepped behind the screen. Kirsten's dress was there, and
another nightgown, but not Maj's dress. He pointed that out
to Luke. He picked up the nightgown and instinctively put it
to his nose. "She wore this," he said, tossing it aside and
stepping around the screen. Luke looked stunned, and Simon
didn't blame him in the least.

Luke rubbed a hand across his forehead. "She must have
left before I was knocked out, but how? She couldn't get past
me. Why would she?"

Simon inwardly winced at the hurt and confusion in his
friend's voice. He had been walking about the room and now
stopped when he came to the corner of what could only be a
trap door near the doc's house. Pushing away the edge of the
rug used to hide it, he stooped and lifted the door's latch. "I
think this may have been how." He peered into the darkness.

Luke brought a lamp over and handed it to Simon until
he started down the ladder, then he reached up for it. He
dropped to the ground and was out of sight for a few moments, then returned. Once he was again standing in the
room, he dusted his hands. "That is definitely how. It leads
right into Doc's main basement. From there, I imagine she
just walked out."

Neither of them mentioned the why. At least now they
were reasonably sure that they were looking for one female,
not two. Maj would have to come later.

"I don't know," Luke said. "She could have been taken
too and we would be missing clues."

"She could have been, but we do know that Kristen has
not gone on her own. I'm sure if Maj was abducted, she and
Kirsten would be together. If not, and we find Kirsten, we

might find another clue." This proved that Kristen was not voluntarily involved, didn't it? "Up to a midnight ride?" Simon asked after a moment.

"Is there any other kind? My horse is at the livery. I'll meet you at the mercantile."

Nodding agreement, they headed their separate ways, only to meet up shortly afterwards.

"Do you know where you're headed?" Luke asked after they started.

"I don't think they would take her anywhere but Weldon's house. It wouldn't make sense to do otherwise."

"Not sure how much sense figures into it, but that's a good place to start. The question is, why would he kidnap her? They're already engaged."

"Yeah, well, if you consider what went on earlier, maybe Weldon wanted to make sure one of them would be collateral for the other."

"Then he would have Maj," Luke reasoned. They rode in silence for a bit before Luke brought up the point that also disturbed Simon, even if the comment did make him bristle. "There has to be a reason he wants Kirsten. I mean, the man is certainly wealthy enough that he can buy anyone he wants."

After another moment of silence, Luke slowed his animal and stared at Simon. "Weldon has made it clear that he just wants into the family, for whatever reason. It wouldn't be a hardship to exchange one girl for the other. Kirsten seems willing to go along with it."

It was Simon's turn to stare. Was that really what his friend thought? Hadn't Maj said anything to him, just in case he had missed the signs on his own?

"It's just that I can't picture her attraction for Weldon," Luke continued.

"There is a lot of money there." He forced himself to say the words. She wouldn't be the first to succumb.

"You don't believe that, Sime?"

"Nah, just stating the obvious."

"So, if we're not setting off to rescue the fair damsel, just where are we going?" he asked after a few more minutes of silence.

"A rescue would be nice," Simon shrugged. "It might even be necessary." Simon knew he wouldn't leave without

Kirsten, but he also knew that the first order of business was Weldon. "If Kirsten is there, we can check on her, but this is the perfect time to find out more."

"I've heard nothing but praises about the man since I've been here. And when the bank opened, you would have thought he was giving money away from the way some of the townspeople talked."

"He was," Simon said. At Luke's startled gaze, he gave a wry grin. "According to some of the newspaper reports, he was giving away a twenty dollar bill to everyone who opened a savings with his bank."

Luke let out a low whistle. "I'd venture to say that impressed a lot of people, and it is the right denomination. Do you think the bills were bogus?"

"We have no way of knowing. At least, not at this point." He held up his hand, indicating that Luke should be quiet. He could barely detect some odd movements up ahead. They could be animal, but he didn't think so.

After they encouraged their horses to the side of the road, they slid from their backs. Simon tied his horse's reins to a low branch and held his hand out, fingers splayed and pointing upward, silently telling Luke to wait five minutes. If he didn't hear or see him in that time, he should come looking for him.

Instinctively checking his gun belt and holster, he sprinted near soundlessly through the woods.

He didn't have to go much further before the subdued voices carried to him. He couldn't tell if they were Weldon's men, but they were definitely up to something they didn't want anyone else to know about.

He could barely make out four men with hats pulled low and bandannas around the bottom half of their faces. Since it wasn't windy, it had to be because they did not want to be seen. The added disadvantage from his point of view was that many of their words were muffled, but the one voice sounded familiar.

"This has to be ready for tomorrow night," the one man said, trying to seemingly hurry two of the others along.

"That just don't make no sense," the shorter man said, all the while continuing to move the dirt so the other man could get the post digger in far enough.

"Who ever heard of digging holes and settin' a fence at

night?"

The other men chuckled along with him until the one pointed out that he was getting well paid for the job.

"Can't hardly see what I'm doing. Those cattle will be through that fence in no time."

The taller man clapped the other on the shoulder. "I do believe that's the plan. Spook one cow and, the next thing you know, you have a stampede on your hands."

The shorter man stopped what he was doing. "But that road leads straight down to the railroad."

"Exactly. Let's get the job done, boys."

They worked in silence for a few minutes, which gave Simon a chance to actually consider their words. He hurried back to Luke to share the information.

"Sounds like he's doing his best to get rid of you," Luke said.

"Sure does. But the question is, why? I already agreed to work for the man. According to the men, the trail will lead to the railroad. There's always potential damage to the trail and the tracks themselves."

"You *are* the railroad to them, Simon. In their opinion, whatever you say or send in your report to the railroad headquarters will have a bearing on what happens for Weldon."

"Wouldn't it make more sense if I was in his pocket, so to speak? He wanted me to make the transfer, to arrange it. You would think he would want to keep me alive to continue."

Luke chuckled. "Well, it seems that he feels he only needs you to do it once. After that, it's ready to go."

Mounted again, Simon smiled and shook his head. Some of these plots never ceased to amaze him. The promise of wealth drove people to incredible lengths. Now, to find out where Kirsten was being kept. This time, he and Luke circled Weldon's property.

Getting close enough to the house was a little more time consuming than he could have wished for, but they made it without being seen. Once they had tied the horses and moved in, they found a few nearby rain barrels to move under the windows so they could gain enough height to peer in.

With Weldon's men about the grounds, they had to move quietly, which meant proceeding slower than Simon would have liked. The first few windows they peered into yielded nothing. Through a window at the back of the house, they spotted Weldon talking to some man. With the shadows, it was difficult to place him, but he looked familiar to Simon. He strained to hear, but he couldn't make out any of the words clearly through the glass.

Luke was stretching his neck, looking into other windows, when he hissed that Simon should join him. At first, he couldn't see what his friend was talking about, but when Luke kept pointing to the comer of the room, he looked again. Cupping the side of his face to block out the moonlight, he could just make out a body in a chair wrapped in blankets. He whistled in air as he realized it was, indeed Kirsten. Talk about bold. He wanted to go in now and take her away, but in all honesty, he realized that she was probably safe enough. He couldn't see anything happening before tomorrow.

Still, there was a niggling doubt. After all, Weldon and her uncle did know that Simon was somehow involved and that he and Kirsten were friends. Pushing away from the window, he jumped lightly off the barrel, landing on the balls of his feet. "Change of plans."

Luke came down much more slowly. "Now why did I think you were going to say that?" He brushed his hands against each other.

"I'm going in," he said, brushing the dirt off his suit.

"Just like that?" Luke didn't bother looking at him, but removed his pistol from its sheath and checked the chambers. Seeing it loaded as it should be, he slipped it back in.

"Actually, I'm going to walk back with you to the horses, then I'm going to ride in. You are going back to town."

"Maybe you should think this through a bit more."

Simon hid a smile and started walking in the direction of the horses. As if Luke wasn't always saying those words, or similar, to him. He was a man of action. That didn't mean he didn't consider what Luke had to say because there was no one, absolutely no one, whose opinion he valued more.

"Listen," he said when they reached the horses and untied the reins, "as long as Weldon thinks I work for him, I shouldn't have any problem getting onto the property and into his house." He pointed his finger and jabbed Luke in the chest. "You, he will know was somehow involved with Maj and, in this case, that could be dangerous. It wouldn't take much for anyone to put everything together and figure that Maj could have confided in you, especially if she was gone when they a ready arrived." They mounted the horses before Simon spoke again. "Besides, he has no need to trust you, nor does he need you."

"You think he trusts you?"

"Hell no. If he did, would he be setting up a stampede ambush? But I think he needs me, at least for the next twenty-four hours, so I plan to make those hours count."

Luke nodded. "I'm going to telegraph Washington to let them know the plan is still in motion."

"If you can figure out how not to let that stampede happen, that would be good, too."

Luke chuckled at that. "I just bet, but I do have a plan or two. It might require a few more men though—another reason for the telegraph."

As Simon suspected, he was not stopped other than for a greeting as he rode through the front gates of Weldon's property.

Once he was announced, Weldon came out of the parlor alone, carrying a glass of spirits with him. "You're a day early, Mr. Barr," he said before taking a sip of his drink.

"Yes, well, I was passing by. Coming back from Pine Grove, you know, so I thought I would stop in and make sure everything is in place."

"Fine, fine," he said. "You come on in here and have a drink."

"Don't mind if I do," Simon said, removing his hat and following the man inside.

"This really is a nice house you have here," Simon said. And it was indeed. Well proportioned. Most of the artwork on the walls was the real thing and in quite good taste.

"Port?" Weldon asked as he headed to the credenza.

Simon followed. "Please." He looked about. This was not the same room that he and Luke had looked in on, but it was on the same side of the house. Presumably, that room was right next to this one. He didn't want to make any moves until he knew for certain.

Weldon didn't offer him a seat, which Simon took to be a good sign. That meant that the man was on edge. Nervous men made mistakes. Simon sipped his drink and watched

Weldon for a tell. "Do I need to know anything for tomorrow?"

Weldon started, but covered it rapidly. "Tomorrow?"

"You did say I was to have an extra stop for the train..."

"Oh, that. Yes. Forgot."

Simon doubted it. "I heard from the office and it won't be a problem. One of the advantages of personnel." He smiled and raised his glass in a silent toast.

Weldon chuckled. "I thought that might be the case. Now my men will have everything ready. All you need do is present yourself to the conductor so that he does know it's all above board."

So the stampede would have to be after the delivery. "I did say that I already spoke to the office. They will have informed the conductor."

"Just trying to be careful here. But it will only take a moment."

Simon took a sip of his drink. "You know, you still have never told me exactly what it is that you wanted from me. I mean, I don't want to have to be responsible for blowing up a train or something like that." He tried to inject the right amount of curiosity and cautiousness in his tone. Truthfully, he didn't care what he did as long as he got the job done—correctly, by his standards. Whatever Weldon was planning would not be correct in Simon's book.

"Nothing like that," the man blustered. "No, no. Just trying to find the quickest way to get things moving."

"Of course." Simon drained his glass and set it on the credenza. "If you have nothing else for me tonight, sir...?"

"Er, no. I'll see you tomorrow." He clapped Simon on the shoulder and guided him to the front door.

Simon half expected to feel the man's boot connect with his backside. They were at the door. In fact, Simon's hand was extended to take hold of the knob when they both heard a crash. Instinctively, Simon turned toward the noise, as did Weldon. When the other man made no immediate move, Simon sprinted toward the sound. He heard Weldon's heavy steps behind him.

"I'm sure it's fine, Mr. Barr," he said.

Simon didn't answer. The sound had come from the room beyond the one he was in. He instinctively slipped one hand to the pistol on his hip and entered the room sideways, staying close to the wall. Weldon immediately followed and ran toward the corner of the room where Simon had spied Kirsten earlier. She was definitely awake now.

The maid looked at Weldon, fear etched on her features. "I just brought in a tray with tea and ham," she said, her voice trembling.

"Then what was the infernal racket?"

"That was me turning over the tray!" Kirsten spoke clearly.

Simon put his gun back in its holster and crossed his arms, watching the little drama unfold. She hadn't seen him yet. At least she wasn't bound; he hadn't been certain earlier. From the clarity of her voice, he would venture to guess the drug had worn off.

She rose from the chair and advanced toward Weldon. "You have some explaining to do," she told him in a not-so-gentle voice. "What am I doing here? I want to go home now."

Simon hoped that she was using that figuratively and didn't remember she didn't exactly have a home at the moment.

"Now, Kirsten, you know a man needs to take care of his fiancée."

"Fiancée?" She lowered her voice.

Simon could practically see her swallowing her words. Good girl.

She started to open her mouth, but spied Simon. Her eyes widened. "What are you doing here?"

"I stopped by to see if Mr. Weldon needed me before tomorrow evening."

Her eyes narrowed as she looked from one man to the other. That wasn't a good sign. He spoke before she had a chance to. "Well, Mr. Weldon, seeing that I'm heading back to town, why don't I just take Miss Bentzer with me. That will save you a trip."

"No," she said.

He gave her a warning look from behind Weldon's back.

"Now, that's not necessary," Weldon chuckled. "I don't mind going out at all."

"Oh, but I insist," Simon said as he reached out and grasped her arm in a vise-like grip.

She stepped closer to him, but addressed Weldon. "On

second thought, that's fine with me. I know how busy you are."

Not giving Weldon a chance to say anything more, Simon steered her toward the door, walking as quickly as possible without seeming to run, even though that was what he longed to do.

"I'll be calling on you tomorrow," Weldon told her as they opened the door.

She merely nodded.

Simon didn't say a word. As soon as they were clear of the steps and he reached for the horse's reins, he jumped on the beast's back and reached down, extending his hand. She put one stockinged foot on his boot and he launched her on to the horse's back behind him. His "hold on" was terse. He kept a sedate pace until he was off the grounds and then eased the horse into a flat out gallop.

"What's the hurry?" she asked from behind him.

He wished he didn't notice her breath skating across his cheek. He didn't bother to answer. He was relatively certain that he was worth more to them alive at this point, but there was no sense in taking chances.

Chapter Eight

Simon didn't rein in his horse until they reached the mercantile. Dismounting, he slid to the ground, insisting that Kirsten stay where she was for the moment.

He gave one thump on the door and it was immediately opened by Luke. "Listen, I'm going to take the horse to the livery, then I'll be back."

"Trouble?"

"As always." Simon grinned at him, then went back to his horse and assisted Kirsten to the ground. He gave her a swift kiss on the top of her head before pushing her toward Luke and throwing himself back in the saddle and heading for the livery.

He slipped into the back of the mercantile in time to see Luke and Kirsten having coffee. Luke held out a mug for him, which he waved away.

"What were you doing?" Kirsten asked. "Luke told me how you found me. Where's Maj?"

"One question at a time," Simon said. "I was doing my job." He loathed telling her what he had really been doing. Even if he trusted her completely, it was not something to be blurted out. "The question here is why did Weldon feel he had to abduct you?"

"As his fiancée, one would think he had every right to see you any time," Luke said.

"Don't call him that!" She bit the words out. "He's a hateful man, totally lacking in integrity."

"Yet your uncle is doing business with him. Perhaps he is more accommodating to his business partners." *Honor among thieves and all that might be more on the mark*, he thought.

"Nonetheless," Luke continued, "he could have seen you anytime, even before he decided you should be his bride." His gaze never left her face.

"He might not have been certain where to find her," Simon said dryly. He pulled out one of the chairs and turned it around so that he could straddle the seat.

Luke chuckled and turned back to his coffee pot. "There is that."

"Where is Maj? She wasn't with me at Weldon's. He made that very clear." She looked from one man to another when they exchanged glances. Shakily, she rose from the chair, keeping one hand on the back. "There's something you're not telling me. I can see that." She turned to lock her gaze with Luke's. "Has something happened to her?"

"We don't think so," Simon said.

She whirled to face him when it was evident that Luke had nothing to say. "What does that mean?" she asked sharply.

Simon rose from the chair and took a step closer to her, hand outstretched to lie on her shoulder. She jerked away from him, and he let his hand fall to his side. "She was gone when I got to you."

She turned on Luke to glare at him, then back to Simon. "I trusted you." She gulped back tears. "You said anyone would have to go through you or Luke, and I believed you!" She plopped back into her chair and propped her elbow on the table, letting her head rest in her hand. "I trusted you."

Simon felt every one of her words as a heavy weight on his shoulders. He stooped down next to her, one hand braced on the back of her chair. She ignored him, but he refused to consider how painful that was. He resisted touching her. A quick glance in Luke's direction showed him just how miserable the man felt; Simon knew he would hold himself to blame. "Kirsten, Luke was unconscious when the men came here," he told her slowly, "but regardless, Maj was already gone."

She didn't lift her head, but she stilled so he knew she was listening. Quickly, he went over the facts as he and Luke knew them. "That's why she wasn't at Weldon's."

"She had no where to go. That makes no sense."

"You said that she needed money to leave. Maybe she felt she had enough." He refused to look at Luke. No matter what, he knew what the other man felt for Maj was much more than a passing fancy and he was taking her disappearance hard.

Nodding, Kirsten sat back in her chair, wiping her eyes with the back of her hand. Simon took out a clean handkerchief from his jacket and passed it to her. "I can't stay here Weldon will find me."

Simon noted the edge of panic in her voice. He didn't want to say or do anything that would push her further along that line.

"Not if he doesn't know where you went," Luke calmly pointed out.

"He knew that I left with Simon, and everyone knows that he is staying at the Grand Hotel."

"True. But I wonder if they're aware that my aunt has also come to stay." Simon smiled down at her as he stood.

"Your aunt?"

That certainly got her attention. She shot him a puzzled look, then turned to Luke.

"You know, Simon, that is a wonderful idea!"

She had no idea what he was talking about, but Luke seemed quite animated as he headed toward a trunk in the corner of his room. He lifted the lid and started moving trays and pieces of clothing. Curious, she stood and wandered over, peering over Luke's shoulder, but he didn't seem to mind.

It appeared that he had pots of face makeup, little jars of she had no idea what, and what looked like a nest of human hair. She pulled back.

Seeming to find what he wanted, Luke held up a longish-haired gray wig. "Think this will work?" He tossed the wig to Simon, who neatly caught it.

A large smile broke over his face, and then he tossed it back to Luke. "You do your magic and I'll go find some things in the mercantle." He stepped over to the door separating the living quarters from the store.

"What are you planning to do?" she asked as Luke stepped closer to her.

He gave her a reassuring smile and told her to sit. "You are going to be Simon's Aunt Evangeline."

"I am?" She sat, but looked askance at the wig. "Look, I'm not very good at dress up or play acting."

"You don't have to be," Luke assured her. "You can just keep your mouth closed until Simon tells you otherwise. But with this disguise, he can keep a close watch over you, and you'll have the added benefit of hiding from Weldon."

He didn't need to say anything more. Grabbing a fistful of her hair, she rapidly braided it, wrapping a strand of hair around the bottom to keep it from unraveling. She turned her face up to his.

"Do your worst," she told him.

In spite of her misgivings, she was totally fascinated by the process and by how very deft Luke appeared to be in making the transformation. Where had he learned such skill?

"You must have been in a theatre troupe," she said after he had the wig in place and was in the process of styling it.

"Yes, well, that was one place I had spent some time."

"If I ever get out of this, I just have to do a story about this," she said.

"No," Simon's firm voice floated from the doorway. "That's one thing you won't want to do. Won't need to do," he corrected himself.

"It would be such fun." She abruptly closed her mouth when Luke put his finger on her chin and pushed up. He was trying to add more lines to her face, and he used some strange piece of India rubber over the bridge of her nose.

From the corner of her eye, she could see Simon lay something over the chest, then make his way to Luke's side. She tried not to focus on that blue gaze. Good thing she had enough makeup on, she thought. She could feel herself growing warm, but he would never know if it was from heat or not. Somehow, with Luke touching her face, she felt nothing, but just seeing Simon in front of her made her lose her senses.

She cleared her throat. "So, how is this to work?"

"I'm going back to the hotel shortly, and Luke will bring you along a bit later saying that he picked you up in Pine Grove. There is a room in the hotel right next to mine that has a connecting door. We'll lease that room for you."

She tried not to let her concern show. She didn't know if

she was ready to be alone yet.

Excusing himself, Simon left the back room, presumably to go to the hotel. She wasn't sure that this would work, but the two men radiated positive thoughts. She looked at the dress Simon had picked and wanted to laugh. Luke did.

"Looks just like something a sixty-year-old matron would wear. No wonder it's been hanging here since I opened."

When she finished changing, she stepped around the changing screen in the corner of Luke's room. She brushed down the front of the dress. Did she really look older?

Leading her to the small mirror he had, he held it up for her. She gasped at the change. If she hadn't known it was her, she would have suspected Aunt Evangeline for sure.

Stepping outdoors and making sure that no one was about, Luke invited her out and they slowly walked to the Grand where they found Simon in the lobby.

He immediately came over to greet them, rather loudly, she thought. Then made a show of escorting her to the front desk where he arranged for her room.

It wasn't until she was settled, and Simon had gone to his own room, that she realized she knew nothing of the next step.

Were the men really as they said, or were they shady confidence men? Like the rest of the town she had accepted Luke as he was, a mercantile offering a needed service. Certainly he seemed honest in all of his dealings, but where would he have learned about disguises such as this? And have so much stuff on hand? She wasn't sure that she trusted his story about having been in a theatre troupe. On the other hand, she had nothing to disabuse her of her thoughts.

And what about Simon? That was a very big question. Again, she had no reason not to believe him, but something didn't seem right. He seemed so much...more. As if working for a railroad in the position he held wasn't high level enough!

She was startled from her thoughts by a brisk thump at the door. She jumped and headed for it before she realized that it came from the next room and not the hall. Immediately, the door opened and Simon strode into the room. Surely, the door had been locked.

"You'll be safer in my room tonight," he told her.

She allowed him to take her by the arm and lead her into his room before she could think to say anything.

"You're staying here too?"

"Of course."

When she stiffened next to him, he chuckled. "You can relax, Kirsten. I intend to sleep in that chair, right there," he said, pointing to the stuffed chair near the window. "I'm a very light sleeper, so I'll hear if anyone wants to...er...visit."

"You were a guard, too." She clasped her hand over her mouth as soon as the words were out, even before she saw the wounded look in Simon's eyes, the one he quickly blinked away. That had not been kind. He had explained what had happened, at least what he and Luke had been able to piece together.

He bowed his head in recognition of the direct hit, then made his way across the room. She followed him further in and reached out to place her hand on his arm. "I'm sorry, Mr. Barr. That wasn't called for."

"But true." His voice was even; it was as if she had never made the outrageous accusation.

"Not entirely. I beg your forgiveness." The set of her shoulders relaxed when he gave her a tight smile. Nonetheless, it had reached his eyes.

She looked around nervously, then finally perched on the edge of the bed. Simon had removed his jacket, vest and neckcloth as he walked through the room; she quickly turned away. It wasn't as if she hadn't seen men in shirt collars before, but somehow, the act of getting that way seemed terribly intimate. Especially in a hotel room. Especially with Simon...Mr. Barr.

Once he had laid his outer clothes aside, Simon angled the chair so that he could see both the window and the door, then sat, stretching his legs out in front of him, and settled deep into the chair.

"You better get some rest," he told her, and closed his eyes.

Nodding, even though she knew he couldn't see her with his eyes closed, she stretched out on the bed on her back, extending her legs. She lay that way for a moment, waiting to see if he really was asleep. She felt much too vulnerable in that position, so turned on her side, facing him. She gasped when she saw that his eyes were open and watching her, the blue nearly obscured by the black of his widened pupils.

"I'm...I'm..." She honestly didn't know what she wanted to say.

He gave her a tired smile. "Good night, Kirsten." His voice sounded firm and pleasant.

She heaved a sigh, relieved that he really did not seem put out at having to rescue her tonight. Her eyelids flew open.

"I never thanked you for tonight, I mean at Weldon's," she said.

Simon didn't open his eyes. "You're safe; that's all that matters."

She settled down again, not truly content with that answer. She frowned. It nearly sounded as if she hadn't meant anything to him, just a package to be handled. She didn't care for the feeling. Although she knew that she *shouldn't* mean anything, but remembering his light kisses had made her think differently. Sighing, she settled her head onto the pillow and willed herself to sleep.

What couldn't have been moments later, she felt a hand over her mouth and a very hard, very masculine body pressed against her. Her eyes widened, then even more when the man leaned over her. Then she let out a small sigh of relief. It was Simon.

He leaned close to her ear, cautioning her to be quiet. Then he stood, and pulled her to a standing position near him. "No matter what you hear, do not move from this spot," he whispered to her, pushing her into the corner behind the drapery and next to the chest of drawers. Raising a finger to his lips, reminding her to be silent, he put his hand on her shoulder and pushed down, encouraging her to crouch. She was halfway down when she heard the noise in the hall. She hadn't questioned Simon, but wondered what he had been about. Could it be Weldon, or one of his men in the hall?

She didn't know what she expected, but it wasn't that Simon would slip under the covers of the bed she had just left!

She pressed her hand tightly to her mouth when she heard the door creak open. She wished desperately that she could see what was occurring, but she had promised she would stay hidden. Amazing how much more she could actually hear with her sense of sight curtailed. There were footfalls, but it was as if the person was trying to be very quiet as he moved closer to the bed. From the curtain, she could detect no light from without, so that meant they must not have lit any lamps. She quite clearly heard the click of a pistol, then Simon's voice.

"State your business."

She shivered at the sound. His voice sounded as hard as his body had been. Maybe more so. She would have been ready to tell all, even if she had nothing to say, she thought, and that would be without looking down the barrel of a pistol.

The muted clicking of the boot heels had stopped immediately. Then she heard a scuffle, and a shot. She stood before remembering that Simon had told her to stay put. What if he wasn't the one who had shot the gun? She leaned against the wall and slid back down to the floor. Who was here and why?

"What's your message?"

She released the breath she hadn't been aware of holding when she heard Simon's voice. There was a grunt, then Simon repeated his question. She supposed that meant neither man was dead. That was good, wasn't it?

She heard the gun cock again. "You have to the count of three to deliver that message. One... Two..."

"Mr. Weldon...he wanted you to come out to the ranch,"

"He did? Hmm. I wonder why he didn't just invite me to stay earlier."

"He did...didn't say..."

"Three," Simon said.

Kirsten covered her ears with her hands, expecting the report from the pistol. Instead, she heard flesh on flesh and a resounding thud. There were footsteps again, but this time they were lighter, then someone turned a lamp on.

Simon leaned over the edge of the dresser and moved the curtain aside. "You can come out now," he told her, extending his hand and helping her to rise. Once she stood, he released her hand and moved over to where she saw the man he had been talking to. She started shaking and bit her lips, trying to regain control.

Simon walked over to his bag and reached inside, coming up with a few pieces of rope. He used one to bind the man's hands behind his back and the other to bind his ankles. He used the man's own kerchief to put in his mouth as a gag.

"How does a railroad manager know how to do that?" she finally got out when he was finished.

"Oh, you'd be amazed at what tricks one learns. Now think," he told her, "can there be any reason Weldon would need me back tonight?"

"It can't be for anything good."

Simon snorted at that. "That sounds right. Still, the man has no reason to lie, and I know Weldon needs the railroad."

Taking Kirsten by the arm, he guided her to the connecting door and pushed her through. He left the door open while he gathered his own belongings and followed her. Once inside, he closed and locked the door between the rooms.

"Hopefully, he'll think I've gone," he said.

"But I don't understand why he was here."

"I don't exactly either. At least, not yet, but I intend to find out."

"What exactly do you do for the railroad, Mr. Barr?"

"It's rather difficult to explain," he said, tossing his bag next to the chair. "A little bit of this and that."

"That's what you said earlier. Don't you think you could give me a real interview? This time, about you?"

"No, that's not necessary. I already told you what the railroad needs to accomplish in this area."

She sat on the edge of the bed and studied him for a moment. "But why is it so important? You make it seem, I don't know—personal, I guess."

Simon chuckled. "My uncle does like to keep tabs on what goes on."

"Oh, a relative! Does he own the railroad?"

"Let's say he has a vested interest."

"Maybe I should do a story on your uncle? You could tell me all about him."

Simon sat next to her on the bed. She couldn't decide if she wanted to move closer or further away. The very nearness, the scent of him, drew her, yet she knew he didn't feel the same. He was a man used to being around women. She could tell that with the careful, yet casual manner that he treated her. He leaned back, placing one arm behind her as he rested his weight on it.

"I think it's time we talked more about *your* uncle."

In spite of wanting to move closer to him, she knew it was in her best interest, self-preservation, she thought wryly, to move further away. She straightened and tried to ignore the smile tugging at his lips.

"I don't know what you mean," she finally said, turning slightly to look at him. "You know more than most people do about my uncle." She had told him her uncle was a printer and distributed newspapers. That was fairly self-explanatory. What more could she say?

He shifted his weight and placed his hand flat against her back. She stiffened. "I know about his treatment of you, and your mistaken loyalty to him, but nothing about him. Aside from the fact that I know the men work together, I know more about your fiancé."

Simon long ago gave up crossing his fingers when he told outright lies. The dossier he had on Weldon and her uncle mentioned little about the printer, focusing mostly on the rancher, but as he well knew, no one operated alone. And he already knew, in her uncle's case, he and Weldon were a team. If Weldon was calling the shots, where did that leave Bentzer? He had to bring something to the table, and that printing press easily equaled a steak dinner.

He hoped that she could tell him something soon because, in spite of the blow he delivered, the man in the other room wouldn't be out for much longer. He didn't want her to start talking just when he had to leave.

Running his hand over her back, he imagined that he could feel the welts there from past blows, and had to tamp down his anger. No matter what his inclination, he was not here to worry about Miss Kirsten Bentzer. He had already spent more time with her than he should have; he inwardly winced at the thought.

"You know, your gray hair is doing quite an admirable job of keeping me in line," he said dryly.

She whipped her head in his direction, and seeing the smile on his face, chuckled too. "I forgot about it." She raised a hand and patted the back of her hair as if making sure it was intact.

Simon straightened, then stood. "I can assure you, if I was a sixty-year-old gentleman, I would be quite entranced."

She gave him a tight smile, but didn't say anything, just watched him warily.

"Listen, Kirsten, I have this niggling feeling that there is something about your uncle that you're not telling me."

"What if that were the case? Why does it matter?"

He refused to let his disappointment in her answer show since it would serve no purpose. Obviously, whatever role she played in her uncle's dealings, if he was guilty—Simon tried to keep an open mind—she did willingly. He had a distinct feeling when this was over his heart was going to hurt. That would almost make his sisters laugh. He brushed the thought aside and firmly reminded himself this was merely a job. She wasn't the first person he'd had to protect in the line of work, even if she was the first he truly cared about.

She stood and crossed her arms over her abdomen, then paced the room. "It doesn't matter, really," she told him. "It's not as if he is doing anything wrong. My uncle is mad, as I've told you, but he's harmless."

Simon had his own thoughts there, but kept quiet, turning to follow her. The wig might have disguised her hair, and the makeup, her face, but there was no disguising her slender, youthful shape, especially as she walked. He swallowed hard and concentrated on what she was saying, ignoring how the shrug of her shoulders brought to mind the creamy whiteness of them, and her stride called to mind just how long her legs were when displayed in trousers.

"He's a printer, and has been forever." She shook her head. "Sometimes I think he has ink in his veins, although he claims that is the case with me. It doesn't matter what he's printing as long as he gets to ink the machine and feel it move."

She had his complete attention. "I thought he printed newspapers and posters."

"Oh, he does. But he needs more to keep in business, you know, so he prints anything people want. Special announcements and invitations, of course."

He walked toward her, stopping just in front of her. "I've been in his shop. The only thing that I saw was the huge paper press and stacks of newsprint." He shook his head. "There wasn't anything else."

She gave a light laugh. "Not there, Mr. Barr! You can't do small items on that big press that he has at the office. He does have a small press, just for special work."

"Of course, I should have realized that," he said, half under his breath.

She tilted her head to one side as she studied him.

"You're not a printer, so you might not have realized that."

No, he wasn't a printer, but certainly knew which presses did what. He knew the large presses were quite capable of printing sheets of bills. But there were smaller presses too, and he had to recall that the bills they were looking for were, without a doubt, among the best forgeries they had ever seen. Maybe the man needed the small press for better control.

"No, I'm not. Why would a small press be better?"

"When Uncle Ralph works with smaller plates, he finds it difficult to line them up correctly on the press bed of the larger press." She extended her hands, palms up, then clasped them together, still keeping them horizontal to demonstrate what she was saying.

"When the plate is on a smaller press, the top fits more snuggly and you get an even print."

"I thought you were the reporter?"

"I am." She let her hands fall to her side.

"You seem to know an awful lot about the differences in the presses." He struggled to keep the sinking feeling in his stomach from coloring his words with suspicion.

"Mr. Barr, I am not stupid. I have been around my uncle's presses for the past several years. I have even helped him set the type when need be."

Simon bowed his head. "My apologies. I did not mean to be insulting." He turned slightly away from her so that she wouldn't feel that he didn't trust her. "So, is this press small enough to fit under a bed?" he chuckled.

She relaxed and, in return, when he glanced at her, she said, "It's at the print shop. There is another room in the basement. You may not have seen it." She waved her hand and the thought away. "You would have had no reason to. It's a small press so uncle only does limited work on it. He doesn't run it very often."

More often than she thought if what he suspected was true. There was the fact that money did not exactly seem to be flooding the area, except for the twenties that Weldon so freely handed out. That puzzled him. He supposed that he would find out if there were any larger, or smaller, bills tomorrow night.

Stepping toward the window, he stood to the side. Moving the curtain the tiniest bit, he peered out. It wasn't all that many hours to sunrise. He would need at least a few hours of sleep to function at peak performance tomorrow.

He turned away from the window to find her watching him. Ignoring her questioning look, he pointed to the bed with his chin, and told her to get some rest.

"But I'm quite wide awake now."

"Nevertheless, you should get some sleep. Tomorrow is going to be here soon and you will have enough to do then."

She sat on the edge of the bed and stared up at him. "And what am I to do tomorrow? I mean, am I still supposed to be Aunt Evangeline? Am I to stay locked in this room?"

"Just rest," he told her. "I don't quite have a plan yet, but I will in the morning." As if he had a choice. Unless Luke came up with one.

She eased herself down on the bed while forming her next question. "Aren't you going to rest?"

"Definitely, but I need to take care of a few things first." He could practically see her blushing from where he stood. Let her think he was talking about answering nature's call. What he needed to do was to make certain the fellow in the other room was going to stay out at least for the rest of the night. He wished he knew what Weldon could possibly want. Perhaps it was merely revenge for him carrying Kirsten off. There was no way for him to know that she was with him now. He might suspect, but Simon hoped the presence of Aunt Evangeline would curtail that line of thought.

He headed for the door, and cautioned her not answer it or to let anyone in. He was taking the key with him. Not that he actually needed it, he thought, but sometimes it did make things a trifle easier.

Once he was in his original room, Simon stooped over the man. He was starting to come around. Simon turned him over on his back.

"Why did Weldon send you?" He wasn't certain the man was completely awake yet so he nudged him in the ribs, not all that gently, with his boot. That did nothing to get his attention. Slipping his hand into his jacket, Simon withdrew his pistol and stooped down next to the man. When the gun cocked, the man opened his eyes.

"Thought that might get your attention. Now, why are you here?"

The man made no move to answer. Simon moved the

gun so that it was in line with the man's temple. His eyes widened at that. Good. "Because of Ralph Bentzer?" The man shook his head. Simon had almost wished it was. The man kept his eyes on the gun. That was good. He was more likely to tell the truth.

"Why did Weldon send you? You were looking for me?"

The man's eyes widened even more, but nodded his head.

Simon nudged the pistol closer. He could hear the man whimper behind his gag. "You're sure?"

The man nodded briskly.

Simon flipped the gun back and released the hammer as he moved it away from the man's head and sat back on his heels. This was definitely going to take some thinking! He was already supposedly working for Weldon, why would he have him followed? Did he suspect that Aunt Evangeline and Kirsten were one and the same?

The man's gaze stayed on Simon's loosely held gun. Slipping the safety back on, Simon thrust out his right fist and slammed the man in the jaw. Standing, he put the gun back in his jacket, then reached for his handkerchief and the small bottle he had slipped in his pocket from his bag. Dousing the handkerchief with the foul smelling chloroform, he held it to the man's nose and mouth, letting him breathe in. He counted to ten, but didn't need to; the man's body relaxed before he got to seven. Certain the man was out, he stood and tucked away his things. That should take care of him, at least until the sun was high and they were gone.

Locking the door behind him, he slipped into the hall and into the adjoining room. A glance at the bed showed Kirsten soundly sleeping. He sat in the chair, and eased off his boots, but kept them in easy reach. He was fairly confident what was left of the night would be peaceful, but you never knew.

When he awakened, he washed his face and hands as quietly as possible. A shave would have been nice, but at least he was able to slip on a clean shirt from his bag. By the time he was completely dressed and groomed, minus the shave, Kirsten was starting to stir. She had raised one very good question—what were they going to do with her?

Ideally, he would like to set her on a train east and out of whatever was going on here, but that was highly unlikely. Besides, he still couldn't be one hundred percent certain that she was not involved in some way. The next best place would be Weldon's. She would be in plain sight, essentially. And because of whatever hold the man had over her, Simon was certain he would not harm her. The question was, how would he feel about taking her back after Simon took her away? Even Luke was going to think he was insane, but how could explain his own sense of dread at leaving her there? Luke would say he was too involved in the case. Simon knew he would put his job first. He was certain of it.

As soon as Kirsten awoke, he told her of his decision for her to go back to Weldon's.

"I thought you said it wasn't safe there."

Simon tried to ignore her rumpled appearance. It certainly added to the aging process, but didn't disguise that it was still Kirsten. "At the moment, I think it's the safest place for you, unless you want to go back to your uncle's." He watched her carefully, not sure what her reactions would tell him.

"Weldon will tell Uncle Ralph that I am there."

"It shouldn't matter at this point," he told her. "I don't think Weldon is going to give you up. He'll protect what is his." He was confident of that or he wouldn't be able to bear sending her back to him, even for the short while that would be necessary.

She didn't look very pleased about that. "You know I don't want to marry the man." She sat up and swung her legs over the edge of the bed.

Simon stood in front of her and took her hands in his, looking into her green eyes and trying not to lose himself in their clear gaze, remembering what his job was and that she might play a larger part in it than he hoped. So far, she had done nothing to earn his trust, but his heart seemed to be on its own path. Mind and heart did not make for a comfortable war. His indecision must have shown on his face.

"What is it, Simon?"

He clasped her hands. "Do you trust me?" His gaze searched hers, looking for any sense of doubt, anything that might show she was not being honest with him.

"Of course, I do."

Simon scoffed. "You say that too easily, m'dear. I want to know that if I tell you to lie in front of a team of careening horses, would you trust that I have my reasons, and that I would save you? That I would never harm you willingly."

She swallowed hard and stared at him. Her gaze was a little troubled, but mostly clear. That had probably not been the best scenario to present to her, but that's what his life felt like at the moment. He wanted to know she wouldn't balk no matter what. The fact that she looked troubled eased his mind somewhat; he knew she took his question seriously when she clasped his hands in turn. "I don't know why I should, Simon, but I do. I trust you implicitly."

He leaned over and gave her a quick kiss on the cheek, then, dropping her hands, stepped away. She had to know that he really didn't want her at Weldon's. He knew one thing for sure. He certainly was not going to be the one to take her there. He couldn't. "We have to go to Luke's first, so I would rather you freshen up there." He assisted her off the bed to stand squarely in front of him.

She raised her chin a notch. He could see she was ready to protest; he headed her off. "If you wash here, it's going to be difficult to explain how Aunt Evangeline became so young overnight." He gave a slight smile when she looked at him as if she had forgotten that fact. He was sure she had. He cupped her elbow as he led her to the door. "A few more moments and this charade will be behind us." And a new one to soon follow. Unfortunately, she would be unaware of it. He pushed the thought from his mind, hoping that he wouldn't find she was in the midst of the counterfeiting ring. His loyalty was hard earned and, once given, was a hard to dislodge, but his heart told him one thing about Kirsten and the logical part of his brain warned him otherwise.

It was early enough and dark enough when they stepped outside that most town folks were not about. In fact, if Simon had not been so sure-footed, there was no telling where they would have ended up.

"We could have waited until full daylight," she hissed at him as they waited outside the mercantile door. It took a moment before Luke opened it.

Simon ushered her in, noting how she took in Luke's appearance. He still wore the same clothes as the day before, a good indication something had caught his attention.

Simon tossed his hat on the small chest and made himself at home while preparing coffee. He insisted Luke and Kirsten have a seat while he pulled three mugs from the shelf and quickly brought Luke up-to-date on the evening's events. He tried to gloss over the uninvited guest, but Luke stopped him, asking where the man was at the moment.

"In my room," he said, pouring the coffee before placing the pot on the table and taking a seat. "Of course, he may have managed to escape by now, but that's where I left him."

"You have no idea where he came from? Who sent him?"

Simon gave a warning look in Kirsten's direction before he answered. "I have some idea. If they're not directly from the ranch, then they might be one of the men we saw earlier." He ignored Kirsten's puzzled look. If she didn't know about the men planning the stampede, so much the better. That was a point in her favor. He played with the cup, twisting it one way and another when he set it back on the table. Anything but look at his partner who was going to think he was insane with his next pronouncement—that Kirsten should go back to Weldon's. He elaborated on the benefits before meeting Luke's gaze.

Luke peered up at him from beneath a furrowed brow as he ran his hand through his hair, rumpling it further. "Let me get this straight. You want Kirsten"—he pointed to her—"to go back to Weldon's." He jerked his thumb in the direction of the ranch. "The same place that you thought she had to leave last night?"

Chapter Nine

"I'm going to get cleaned up." Luke finished his coffee, pushed himself away from the table, stood and headed to the other side of the room where he had set up another screen to block off his sleeping area.

That was fine with Simon. Kirsten had earlier removed her makeup and wig with Luke's assistance and then had cleaned herself up. There was nothing much Simon could say until she was out of earshot, and in the small room, that was pretty much nowhere.

"Are you taking her back?" Luke had asked.

"Do I look insane?" Although he began to wonder if he wasn't just that; not for taking her to Weldon's now, because he did believe that she would be safe enough, but at his actions the night before in even removing her. "I think I'll see Weldon soon enough. I'll walk her to the livery and arrange for transportation there." He nodded yes to Luke's unvoiced question.

That would be a good a place as any to meet, and they would be able to get their mounts.

Once Luke tied on his apron and entered the mercantile through the connecting door, Simon stood and held out his hand to Kirsten. He knew there was no reason for him to touch her, except that he couldn't seem to stop himself. That was definitely not good. It sounded as if his brain was losing the war and that could not be. Not at this point. They were closing in on the end of the chase; he could feel it. He sternly reminded himself that he only had to stand firm against any attraction he might feel for Kirsten a short while more, then he would know where the chips would fall.

They walked to the livery mostly in silence. It was still early for walking around, but there were more people about than when they had set out for the mercantile; he insisted that she walk in the shadows of the building. The less people who saw her about, the better. No need for an encounter with her uncle should he be about, or for anyone to inadvertently carry tales back to him.

As he was about to step into the livery, she grabbed his arm. He looked down at her in surprise. "What is it? Are you afraid?" *Don't let it be that.* He knew it was in her best interest to be at Weldon's; it was the safest place aside from the jail, but he didn't want to frighten her unduly. Besides, he still didn't know if he could trust her.

"You asked me if I trusted you." She had removed her hand from his arm and looked at him steadily. "Now, I'm asking you the same. Do you trust me?"

Simon drew his brows together. What was she planning that would make her ask such a question now and not earlier? Had she been able to read his mind, his face, that easily? If he said yes, would it be admitting that he believed she was innocent? "Why wouldn't I trust you? What are you planning?"

She gave him a tight smile at that. "I'm not planning anything. I don't know, I just wanted reassurance, I suppose. I haven't known you long, but since last night it seems as if you are holding back. I thought maybe you didn't believe me, the things I've said, not trusted me."

He had been more intense in his actions since last night, more focused, but he hadn't believed that would be noticeable to her. "Kirsten, I only trust a select few people." Aside from his family, he could think of only one, Luke. He would love to add her to the list, but he couldn't do that just yet. What kind of man did that make him?

He noticed the sheriff walking toward the hotel, and abruptly discontinued that thought. Turning to block her from sheriff's view, or any others, he leaned close and practically whispered, "Listen, when you get to Weldon's, be careful who you talk to or what you say." He didn't think whether or not he should warn her. He just did it. She was an intelligent woman and he hoped that he hadn't tipped his hand by forewarning her. Even if his brain insisted that she could be part of it, his gut refused to believe it.

There was no disguising the instant puzzlement on her face. "I don't care for Weldon, not enough to be married to the man, but he is a friend of my uncle's. I'm sure he's all right. I mean, you make it sound dangerous and I'm sure Greg is not."

Suddenly, the thought that she trusted him was knocked down a peg. Not that it mattered. And she called Weldon by his given name, one of the few times he had heard her do so. Even if she wasn't involved, he was certain her uncle was. It felt like it fit, without even going into the evidence that could prove it so. Evidently, in spite of his treatment of her, she had some feeling for the man. "Things are not always as they seem," he told her.

"They seldom are," she agreed, "but I don't know why that is a problem here. I've known Weldon for a long time. I can't say that I ever cared for him, but, really, I never paid any attention to him. To me, he was a friend of my uncle." She gave him a wry smile. "I met him before Maj and I moved here. Truly, there were happier times and we would visit my uncle. My family was in the press business, too, so there was always something to share."

Most likely, she trusted Weldon more than himself no matter what she had to say about the man. It wasn't unusual for familiarity to build trust. What a web. He leaned over and gave her a quick peck on the cheek. It was all that he would allow himself. "Just be careful."

The livery was fairly deserted when Simon guided her in and then called for the manager. He quickly made arrangements for her to ride to Weldon's ranch.

"Hey, you're that fancy railroad guy my partner was talking about."

"Right. Is that a problem?" Simon kept his voice even, but it was good to know what people were thinking.

The man chortled as he went about readying a buggy. "Not at all. Was wondering if you found out what you needed. This town could use more stops, you know. Once every other week just isn't enough for business."

"No, I didn't know." Aside from the one that Weldon desired, he couldn't see many people stopping at Hobart. It was nice little place, but no different than many other towns.

"Let me get a driver," the man said as he wandered off.

Simon glanced at Kirsten to see a smile tugging at the comer of her lips. The little man had been amusing. "Why would anyone want to stop here?"

"Maybe he can tell us," Simon said as the man came bustling back.

"Driver will be out front in a moment, soon as I get this here horse harnessed."

Simon gave him a hand in holding the traces while he harnessed the horse.

"Thank ye. Most city folks don't know one end of the horse from the other." He chortled at his own joke.

"You get many city folk here?"

"Now and then. People come to Weldon's ranch, you know."

He did now.

"And when they was getting plans for the bank and building it—lots of activity."

After leading the equipage out, the driver hopped in and held the reins. Simon assisted Kirsten into the buggy, reminding her that he would see her shortly, then tapped the buggy side, indicating she should move on.

He followed the man back into the livery, and requested Luke's horse as well as his own. The plan was that he would meet Luke here and have the horse already saddled.

"Forgot you were a friend of Mr. Hayden. Sure was glad he opened that store."

Simon was beginning to feel guilty that it was all a ruse. So many people seemed genuinely happy about it. "Well, I'm sure someone would have come along."

"True, true, but better sooner than later, if you know what I mean. We always need things out here. This close to the railroad, we get deliveries to the store pretty quick."

"I can see where that helps." Simon hefted his saddle on the horse's back while the man finished putting on the bridle.

"Now, when you write that report, you tell them what a great town this is, right?"

"Oh, definitely," Simon said.

"It's a good thing that Mr. Hayden has friends in high places, right?"

More right than he knew, and it wasn't himself he was

thinking of. Tossing the man a coin, Simon led both horses out in time to see Luke walking down the street.

Once mounted, they didn't speak of anything much until they were nearly a mile out of town. Sometimes it was simply best to speak where no one would accidentally overhear them. "I really, really don't like this, Simon. We don't seem any closer to the solution to this puzzle."

"We're a lot closer than we were, but there is something not quite right," he agreed. "I have no idea exactly what Weldon is planning to do with the delivery tonight. Is it going to be real bills or counterfeit?"

"Rather wondering about the proposed stampede, myself."

"There is that."

Both men lapsed into silence before Luke mentioned another point. "I did hear that there is going to be bank wagon bringing deliveries to the bank this afternoon."

Simon sharpened his gaze and sat up straighter in the saddle. "From where?"

"That's what I'm waiting to hear. I'm anticipating a telegram later this morning. The Treasury is to let me know where their shipment is headed."

"If it's here, it will have to be real bills," Simon muttered. "This is the perfect time for him to make the switch from real to bogus. The hard part will be determining if that truck is empty or full. If it's full, I don't know if we can risk blowing up real greenbacks. Somehow, I just can't picture the President approving of that."

Luke chuckled. "Guess I was thinking too far ahead of myself. I was thinking that, if the truck carried counterfeits, we could be doing everyone a favor just blowing it up."

"On Main Street?" Simon asked.

"You have a better idea?"

There was silence for a few moments, each man trying to come up with a better scenario.

"Actually, I think we need to see what's in it or not, for certain, before making that decision. Destroying real greenbacks could be a problem."   "True." Luke shifted in his saddle and looked at the sky. "It's about time for me to open the store. If there's a message from Washington, we'll know what to do."

"Right," Simon said, turning his horse. "And if not, I'll just have to have a look inside the wagon."

"On Main Street?" Luke mimicked his partner's earlier tone of voice.

Simon chuckled. "It won't be a problem since you'll be able to provide a diversion." With that comment, he urged his horse forward and started to canter toward town.

Once they were back at the mercantile, Luke flipped the sign to "open" while Simon waited to see if there was a new message from Washington. After a second cup of coffee as he waited and plotted his next move, he poured another mug full and took it out to the front of the store where Luke played shopkeeper. It appeared there would be no early morning message.

Luke reached for the coffee gratefully. "You had that timed so as not to run into Mrs. Isabelle again," he teased.

"Did I? Really?" Simon managed to look somewhat surprised. He looked around at the merchandise Luke had stacked on the shelves. "You know, you look pretty comfortable here, Luke. Ever think of settling down?"

"In one place?" There was no disguising the surprise in his voice. "Not sure I could do it."

"Maybe not one place, but at least going home—when you went home—to the same person."

"Yeah, that does cross my mind once in a while." He took another sip of the coffee, and then started. They both heard the clattering of the telegraph key from the other room.

"Shall I get it, or you?"

"I see Mrs. Brown heading up the street. You better get it," he told Simon.

Stepping into the back room, Simon leaned over at the telegraph and keyed that he was present and was waiting for the rest of the transmission. He wrote it down hurriedly, but unless Luke was busy with a customer, he would have already heard it. The Treasury was not making any deliveries.

"Then it has to be an empty truck intending a pick up," Luke said when they were alone again. "There's no other explanation."

"I agree, but how best to put it out of commission?"

"Blow it up?" he asked, referencing their earlier discussion.

Simon chuckled. "You do love your toys, Luke, but too many people can be hurt. If we could disengage the horses..."

"Brilliant, Simon. I only need a moment to get to the harness."

"Better yet, you engage the driver in conversation and I'll slip under the wagon and release the horses."

Luke nodded slowly. "That could work, but how are we going to keep them from moving the money from the safe to the wagon?"

Simon smacked his forehead with his hand. "What am I thinking? The answer, Luke, is to get into the bank and the safe before the wagon ever gets there."

"Except for the small fact that the wagon will be here this afternoon, and the bank will have customers..."

"True." Disappointment colored his voice. "The other alternative is that we could blow the wagon up quietly."

Luke burst into laughter. "What the devil do you mean?"

"Instead of blowing it up, maybe you could start a small fire, or a loud diversion." He waved his hands about. "You know with firecrackers, or whatever it is you use."

"Now that's a perfect solution." Luke rubbed his chin, seeming to consider the scenario. "We just need to decide how to do that while the guards are sitting on the top of the box. It will be a challenge." There was satisfaction in his voice.

"Thought you might see it that way," Simon said. Glancing at one of the clocks Luke had on display in his store, he said, "That delivery should be here in about two hours. I'm going to the hotel and then will head over to the bank shortly before the wagon is due to arrive."

"I can leave the store about that time and make my deposit. I'll be fully equipped, of course."

Simon grinned at him. As if there was any doubt! He might have made the comment in jest, but the truth was that Luke did indeed enjoy his diversions. He kept up to date on all of the latest gadgets, even though they seemed to be appearing at an alarming rate. Simon was fascinated, but was willing to trust the information from Luke on any new advancements that might help them in their line of work.

Back in the hotel room, Simon checked the assorted weapons on his person, swept his hat off the dresser and put it on his head before leaving for the bank. It appeared that the armored truck was scheduled to arrive at the Weldon

Bank & Trust at the busiest time of the day. They certainly seemed to have everything planned exactly right and took all precautions.

Although he had spent most of his time in Hobart blending into the shadows, Simon made sure he was seen today. He slowly walked along the town sidewalks, smiling politely to anyone he encountered. The idea was to move slowly and be seen, even if it was against his nature.

Wandering inside the bank, he greeted the few people he had come to know by sight and got behind a man who was taking his time about completing his transaction.

"I can take you over here," the teller at the next window said.

Simon gave him a smile and gritted his teeth. Just what he needed—a helpful person. Any other day the man probably would have ignored him.

"What can I do for you?"

"I'd like to cash this check," Simon said, "but I'm not sure I trust those Federal greenbacks just yet. What else does the bank have?" In a time when every bank had the right to make their own currency, people were still able to request other bills. Some of the banks liked to carry different denominations in different currency.

The teller leaned conspiringly near the window. "Mr. Weldon has some five dollar bills, and some twenty dollar bills. The rest are greenbacks."

Simon pretended to be disappointed. "No Smiths."

"'Fraid not. Heard those were some nice-looking bills, but not too many of them in these parts. Maybe once Mr. Weldon gets regular delivery with the train."

"The train?" Simon tried to keep his voice to merely curious. What regular delivery? Did townspeople know about the unscheduled, supposedly secret, stop?

"Yes, sir. He's making connections so that the train will stop on his property..." The man trailed off and looked at Simon more closely. "That's information only for employees, you know, but since you're that train guy...Well, I figure you know already since he said you were working for him." The teller peered over his glasses at him.

They did know! *What had the man been thinking to allow so many in on what was essentially a crooked deal?* "Did he now?" Simon shifted his weight and brought out his wallet, indicating that he would like to get to the business at hand.

"Oh, yes, your money." After confirming the amount, the teller went back to hastily counting it out in Weldon bills when Simon stopped him.

"On second thought, I'll take some of the greenbacks, even though the Weldon bills look nicer. I'll be leaving the area soon and some places prefer greenbacks," he stated at the man's sharp look. That much was true. Besides, it wasn't the Weldon bills they were worried about. The Treasury department had those accounted for. It was the supposed Federal greenbacks in twenty dollar amounts that had them concerned.

"That they do. The little bit of color makes it look much more attractive," the teller agreed as he switched the lower denomination greenbacks for the Weldon bills.

Taking care to stop at the table set up for customer use in counting money and checking transactions, Simon placed his money in his wallet and tucked the billfold in his pocket, taking at least twice as long as he normally would. He glanced out the window. No sign of the wagon, but since there was no sign of Luke, he supposed that was just fine.

Making his way outdoors, he walked past the hitching post, waiting to see who would show up first, and hoped for his partner.

Luke walked into the bank and completed his transaction quickly, then headed back outdoors to join Simon, following his gaze up and down the street.

"You ready?" Even as Simon asked, he knew it was an absurd question. He had never known his partner not to be ready for any eventuality, even when it wasn't planned. It just wasn't in Luke's make up!

Luke patted his coat pocket, then moved closer to Simon so he could better slip him a few strings of firecrackers without anyone noticing. "Thought it might be good if you had a few too."

Silently, Simon palmed them into his jacket pocket. When he withdrew his hand, he held two cigars, which he extended to Luke, who took one and slipped it between his lips.

"Don't mind if I do."

A nice, friendly gesture, not to mention that the cigars would come in very handy in lighting the string of firecrackers. It might get in the way a bit, but definitely worth the trouble.

The men lit their cigars, each looking in the distance. "I hear them coming up now," Simon said. The heavy wagon and slow plod of the horses slowly made their way up the dirt street.

Nodding agreement, Luke started walking quickly toward the sound. The earlier they could get a look at the wagon, the better the chance they would have of stopping it. Simon was immediately behind his friend, then past him.

The wagon, which wasn't traveling very quickly to begin with, slowed down the closer it got to the center of town. Unlike the wagons from the Treasury, this one did not have Federal soldiers as outriders, and certainly a lot less riders than one would think they needed. There were only two, plus the two drivers.

Simon shot a glance at Luke, who nodded that he was ready when his partner was. Even with only two riders, Luke was going to have to create a diversion immediately and Simon would have to risk getting a look inside on his own.

Casually stepping off the sidewalk, he waited until the outriders passed him, then started to cross the street. As soon as he was level with the back of the wagon, he followed it for a moment. Then, taking out a strand of firecrackers, he lit it with his cigar and gave it an underhand toss to the far side of the street. As soon as the noise caught everyone's attention, including the driver's, he hopped on the back of the wagon.

Most of it was closed except for a few gun slits. He only had a moment to peer in before the horses, drivers, or anyone else noticed that he was on board. Empty. That meant the driver was picking up. Releasing his hold, Simon lightly jumped away from the vehicle. Signaling to Luke that the wagon was empty, he watched as it made its way closer to the bank. They only had moments to make sure that the money didn't leave the bank, let alone get loaded into the wagon.

Taking another strand of firecrackers from his jacket, he turned toward the building, brought his cigar down to light them and tossed them in front of the horses. As expected, the animals shied, causing the drivers to slow down in order to keep the wagon on course. It was enough time for Luke to light and toss one of his small bombs at the wagon. Simon sent another string of firecrackers in front of the outriders who had just got their mounts under control. By now, both he and Luke had moved closer to the group, to blend in, trying to look just as shocked.

People were pouring out of the stores and looking through windows at the commotion. One of the outriders must have recognized Simon because he drew his pistol and aimed in his direction. "Hey, you!"

Realizing that the man knew he had been involved with the disturbance, Simon pushed further into the crowd. Being discovered was not exactly what he needed. Evidently, the man had enough sense not to shoot into the group. Instead, he slid from his horse and started to push his way through.

"Keep moving," Luke hissed nearby.

Nodding, Simon pushed his way through the crowd, confident that Luke would cover for him as much as possible. It wasn't enough, he thought, when he felt a heavy hand on his shoulder. "Stop right there, mister."

Simon swiveled around, fist at the ready, and swung at the man's jaw. The crowd moved away. Instead of retaliating, the man brought his pistol up to Simon's face.

Looking down the black hole of the Remington Army Revolver was all the convincing he needed to stop. There was no way the man could miss at that range. Nor could Simon jeopardize all of the people around him. Immediately, he raised his hands, showing there would be no threat—yet.

"What's going on here?" The sheriff pushed his way to the center of the crowd. "Put that away," he commanded the outrider.

The man lowered his weapon, but didn't return it to its holster. Not a comforting sight.

The sheriff looked at Simon and snorted. "Should have known it was you, railroad man."

Simon lowered his hands and gave the sheriff a questioning look.

"Any time there's anything going on, you seem to be involved."

Simon tried to look modest and shrugged. He doubted that the sheriff was aware of his activities, so the comment surprised him, but he didn't address it for now. At least the mission for today was accomplished. They just had to hope there wasn't another wagon ready to take over if this one failed. Simon doubted it. With this many people looking on, it appeared that the wagon was going to give the bank a miss altogether. "I guess it's a matter of being in the wrong place at the wrong time."

"Funny, I wouldn't put it quite that way. No, sir. Right now, I would say you were in exactly the right place at the right time."

This did not sound much more comfortable than the business end of the pistol.

"'Fraid I'm going to have to put you under arrest." The sheriff moved closer to him and grasped Simon's arm.

Simon gritted his teeth. He really didn't need this at the moment. Especially when he still didn't know if the sheriff was involved or not. There was always that possibility. Nothing seemed to directly point to the man, but he couldn't rid himself of the feeling. It wouldn't be the first time on a case where law enforcement had turned a blind eye for profit. Oftentimes, it was the only way some of the schemes worked. "On what charges?"

"Disturbing the peace will do for a start."

He knew no one had seen him throw those firecrackers.

"You can't be pushing through a crowd of people like that." He pressed Simon in the direction of the jail.

"I was trying to escape a maniac."

"That's not the way I heard it. And then there's the matter of assault. You can't be taking swings at people for no reason."

"He had a gun in my face!"

"Because you ran from him!" The sheriff gave another shove. "That's enough talkin' for now. You can cool off in the jail and then if this here man"—he used his thumb to indicate the outrider—"wants to press charges, you'll have to face that."

By now they were in front of the jail, and the sheriff pushed the door open, and Simon through it. As soon as they were inside, Simon whirled to face the sheriff.

"Now, listen, sheriff. I don't know what you think is going on here—"

"I think you best be quiet and get in that cell before I push you into it."

Simon resisted rolling his eyes and walked into the cell.

He may as well spend the afternoon here and learn what he could, if anything, from the sheriff. Luke would undoubtedly stop by. Yet when he sat down and was free to let his thoughts wander, it wasn't thoughts of the sheriff or his partner that went through his mind, but Kirsten. That wasn't a good sign. He couldn't help but think of her with Weldon. Even knowing that Weldon was a hard man, he was certain he wouldn't physically harm Kirsten the way her uncle had. There might have been other cruelties, but he trusted that she would remain in one piece if for no other reason than Weldon still seemed to want to marry into the family.

A few hours later, close to dinner time, Luke ambled over to the jail.

"I guess there's no reason for you not to talk to him," the sheriff answered to Luke's inquiry. "Just remember, I'll be right outside."

Once he was close enough, after greeting his friend, Luke passed him a slim piece of metal, quite capable of picking the simple jail lock.

Luke looked him over and noticed he still had his jacket. "You are still armed, I take it."

"Except for this," he said, slapping the side of his hip where his holster normally rested.

"Be sure to pick it up on the way out. Now, I better go before he starts getting concerned and thinks I'm helping you to break out." Chuckling, he left the building.

Simon spent most of the next few hours thinking, or trying to push away thoughts of Kirsten and concentrate on what needed to be done to the train.

Right now, he didn't need to be anywhere and it seemed best to stay put. As soon as it was full dark, he intended to leave. In the meantime, he made himself comfortable.

The sheriff stopped by the cell a few minutes later and leaned against the wall.

"So, now, why would a fancy railroad man like you get the bright idea to steal a bank wagon?"

Simon looked at him in surprise. "Steal? Is that what you thought I was doing?"

"Ain't nothin' else you could be doin', spooking those horses and jumping on that wagon. You have a better explanation?"

A lot better, but hardly one he could voice. So, the sheriff had seen him jump on the back. It was a risk he had willingly taken; there was no other way to see what was inside before it arrived at the bank. "I just wanted to see what was inside," he said nonchalantly.

"What, you city folks never seen a bank wagon?" He snorted in disbelief. "No mind about that. Came to tell you I'll be heading out and the deputy will be in to take over my duties. If you need anything, you ask him."

Better yet. As far as he was concerned, the sheriff had been all too closed mouthed about a lot of things. If he had time before the train would be coming in, then he was going to follow him.

"I was supposed to meet with Mr. Weldon tonight," Simon said casually.

"I don't think that's going to happen."

Giving a deep chuckle, Simon agreed. He would have to have known about Simon's meeting. He wondered what Weldon would do if he didn't show up. At one point, he seemed to feel it was necessary that Simon be on hand to meet the engineer. After that, it wouldn't matter, at least that was Simon's take on it if the stampede plans were anything to go by. "But if you do see him by chance, mention that I was unavoidably detained."

The sheriff shot him a suspicious look. "Do I look like an errand boy?"

"No, sir. Just commenting. I didn't want to trouble you for paper and pencil."

The sheriff pushed away from the wall. "No messages unless I read them."

"I have no secrets." He held his hands up, spreading them wide while he was still sitting on the bunk. "But I am curious, sheriff. Why did they move that bank wagon in at the busiest part of the day? I would have thought late at night or early morning would have been better."

"Ain't none of your business, or mine either. Now, I hear the deputy comin' in."

Simon could hear the door opening and boot heels on the wooden floor, but from the angle of the cell, he couldn't actually see the door. He did hear the sheriff giving last minute instructions before heading out. The deputy came in the back to introduce himself. By then, Simon was standing practically against the bars of the cell.

"Work here long?"

"No, sir," the deputy said. He was rather young, maybe early twenties, but he seemed much younger.

"Sounded like the sheriff has quite a list for you."

The deputy shrugged. "No more than usual. Well, except for you. We don't get many real prisoners, just one here and there for disorderly conduct."

"I did hear something to that effect." Simon tried not to let his lips twitch. Either that was the only law the man knew, or he, himself, had just slid to the level of drunkard without even trying.

Nodding to him, the deputy wished him a good night and headed back to his desk.

From here, Simon could see him very well. Unfortunately, it meant that he could also be seen. If the deputy did not fall asleep soon, he was going to have to call him back over.

Half an hour later Simon called for some water.

"I said good night," the deputy said.

"And I said I wanted water." His voice got louder as he repeated it. "Do I need to report you for abuse of a prisoner?" He readied himself when he heard the angry thrust of the chair away from the desk and the deputy coming over.

"Now, see here..."

That was as far as he got. In the next moment, Simon had whipped his hand through the bars and grabbed the man's shirt, hauling him so close their cheeks nearly touched. The deputy started to reach his hand down for his gun, but Simon was ahead of him. He grabbed it and held it under the man's chin.

"Unlock the door."

"Listen, mister, I can have the whole town here in a moment."

Simon cocked the gun and repeated his request. This time, the man fumbled with the keys, but managed to unlock the door. Simon stepped through with his arms still between the bars and the deputy in front.

"Now, I'm going to release you, but one sound, one move, and I will shoot. Understood?"

The deputy wet his lips with the tip of his tongue, but nodded.

"Thought you were a smart man." Simon did as he said, never letting the deputy out of gun sight. Then, the deputy immediately proved him wrong by leaping for one of the rifles. Simon followed. As soon as his hand landed on the deputy's shoulder, he spun him around, his fist connecting with the man's jaw. Taken by surprise, the deputy staggered until he managed to hit his head against the edge of the gun case and slumped on the floor. Shaking his head, Simon stopped over him, making sure he was breathing.

Grabbing the man's bandanna, he thrust it in his mouth, then using a pair of the sheriff's handcuffs, cuffed the deputy's hands behind his back. He stripped the man's belt and bound his feet with it. Finally, he left the deputy's gun on the desk as he picked up his own gun belt and exited the jail. He found Luke on the side of the building, sitting on his horse and holding Barr's Pride by the reins. Simon buckled on his belt as he strode to the horses.

"Took you long enough," Luke said as Simon vaulted into the saddle.

"That it did. A little messier than I planned." Instead of heading toward the ranch, Simon turned his horse to town. "Before we get to Weldon's I want to see what's in the bank."

"Good idea," Luke said. "If we're quick, we should have enough time."

Riding to the back of the bank, the men dismounted and tied their horses to one of the posts. It only took them a matter of moments to break into the building. From his earlier visits, Simon knew exactly where the vault was located.

"You would think there would be more security—okay, at least some security—about," Luke said as they made their way to the safe.

"Either there's nothing worth guarding or they're all at Weldons."

Simon had been positive the safe would be a Lily, and was glad to see he was correct. It was, without a doubt, the best and most safe-cracking proof safe on the market.

"Would you like a go?" he politely asked Luke. They were both good at opening things that should stay locked. Over the years it had become nearly a contest with them to see who could do it faster. By mutual consent, they agreed to take turns.

"Nah. You can go first."

Leaning close to the lock tumbler, Simon listened as it went past the numbers until he heard a click. "There will be no second," he warned his partner, who just grinned at him. By then, Simon was swinging open the door to the safe.

Grabbing one of the lamps on a nearby desk, Luke brought it near, allowing the door and the safe itself to shield its light. "Greenbacks?"

Simon shook his head as he continued to rifle through the bundles of bills. "Not these. Weldon Bank & Trust, every one of them."

"You don't think they're real, do you?"

"You mean backed? No, but they're not the ones bothering me." He reached into the safe again, pushed aside the Weldon bills and brought out a stack of twenty dollar bills. Greenbacks. Simon reached for several random bills and tucked them in his pocket. They would need them for comparison later. He straightened, and Luke extinguished the light.

They exited the building as quietly as they had entered, but were never stopped.

"That's uncanny," Simon said. "Which leads me to believe they know there is nothing here worth protecting." Everyone was probably at Weldon's where the new bills were supposedly passing through.

Turning his horse, he kept him to a trot until they were away from the main street and headed toward Weldon's ranch. He outlined his suspicions about the sheriff.

"Come on, Sime. You have nothing to go on."

"Just my gut, Luke, just my gut."

"Well, I think it's off this time." He looked at the sky. "What time did you say you were to meet the train?"

"Nine o'clock." Looking up at the sky himself, he bit back a curse and urged his horse to a gallop. "Let's head to the meeting point directly," he said before starting off.

Chapter Ten

Kirsten hated being a prisoner. There was no other word for it. Certainly, Weldon was nice; behaved like a gentleman, in fact, even if he was bit rough about the edges. She had lived in different places and met different men, but she had never met a true gentleman before Mr. Barr—and Mr. Hayden. She tried not to dwell on Simon. In spite of Weldon's gentlemanlike manners, she knew it didn't extend to his core. With Simon—and Luke—it was part of who they were.

"Just how did you spend your evening, m'dear?" he had asked her over dinner.

"I had a few errands to tend to." She tried to keep her mouth full, the better not to have to answer him, but he didn't seem to take it as a deterrent.

"I thought you were quite delighted to go off with Mr. Barr."

No sense in denying that, so she didn't. "I hadn't exactly appreciated being kidnapped!" she snapped.

He had the grace to look affronted. "Well, that may have been a mistake, m'dear, but I wanted to be sure you would be in a safe place. I don't exactly trust that railroad man."

He made it sound like being a railroad manager was as bad as a confidence man. She was glad she had just put a piece of potato in her mouth and couldn't speak! Not trust Simon? He seemed the most steadfast person she knew, and that was in spite of some of his strange ways. Even she had to admit there were some things she would like answers to, but his sense of integrity was never one of them. Of the two men, she would trust Simon no matter what.

"Now that I *am* here, of my own free will," she pointed out, though that was far from the truth, "what do you plan?"

"Why, mostly just to enjoy your company. I thought we could take a day or so to know each other better before we marry."

Kirsten dabbed her lips with her napkin. She had no more intention of marrying him than watching the sun set in the east! She brought her attention back to the matter at hand. "I wasn't under the impression we were to marry any time soon."

"The preacher will be through this end of the territory in a few days. Your uncle thought it would best—"

"My uncle can have no bearing on what I do."

"Oh, you're quite wrong, m'dear. Your uncle and I made plans some time ago. Now they have to be adjusted a bit. This really is the better solution anyway."

"If you and my uncle get along so well, then marry him!"

Weldon chuckled. "I do like spirit." He wiped the smile from his face. "But your humor is sadly misplaced and I don't appreciate it."

Pushing her chair from the table, Kirsten stood. "And I don't appreciate your attitude, sir. If you cannot recall, the north has won the war, and slaves are free. I do not need to be your slave." With that, she practically stomped from the room toward the bedroom assigned to her earlier. She didn't care if Weldon followed or not.

Once there, she spent a good amount of time pacing until the sound of a horse riding up to the front caught her attention. From her room, she could make out a single horse and rider. The figure looked familiar as he dismounted, tied his horse, and headed for the door. Since she could tell no more, she sat in the chair near the fireplace and stared moodily into the flames. She tried not to think of Simon, but the harder she tried to banish him from her thoughts, the more clearly his face came to her mind's eye.

In spite of her intention not to, she started to doze off. In that half-asleep, half-awake state, she heard Weldon's voice rather clearly. Then her uncle's. That brought her awake. What was he doing here? She struggled to pinpoint the source of the voices for they sounded as if they were quite near. She couldn't make out the words clearly through the door.

Standing and stretching, she crept silently to the door. She put her ear to the wood, all the while turning the knob, careful not to make any sound. She was barely breathing. Opening the door just enough to be able to peer out, she pressed her face to the wood. The voices had sounded so very close because they were in the same length of hall.

The door to Weldon's study stood ajar. From her angle, she could barely make out her uncle's profile as he accepted a cigar from the other man. There was silence as both men trimmed their cigars, lit their smokes and took the first puff.

"You're sure he's out of the way?" That was Weldon.

"Yeah, I'm sure. The sheriff has him locked nice and tight. The only problem is that I thought you needed him for the train."

"It would have been easier, that's for sure, but he made the necessary arrangements." There was silence for a moment before he continued. "After that fool stunt today I'm not sure that I can trust him."

"What do you think he was really after? He couldn't have wanted to steal anything in the middle of the day. No one is that stupid."

"I have no—" He stopped himself in mid-sentence. "I have a feeling he *wanted* to be thrown in jail."

Her uncle chuckled. "That makes no sense."

"No?" Weldon sounded closer to his own door now so she stepped back and closed hers even more; there was barely a sliver of light. "If he's in jail then he can't be doing anything to jeopardize his job with the railroad now, can he?" Weldon gave an appreciative chuckle. "The man is smarter than I thought. Might have to even give him a bonus tomorrow."

"You're going to keep him?"

"Or kill him."

Kirsten gasped and pulled away from the door. He hadn't sounded as if he was jesting. Weldon was worse than her uncle! To think that he would say such a thing about anyone was horrible enough, but to think that he meant Simon devastated her.

Holding the knob so that it wouldn't click, she let the door close completely. She would like to have stayed, but she didn't think there would be anything more they could add.

She had to warn Simon.

She covered her mouth with her hand to smother any sound she might make as she thought through her options. There weren't many. She took a deep breath, focusing on what she needed to do. Frowning, she wondered why her uncle was even here. She had wondered earlier, but dismissed it until she heard their plans. Could this be why her uncle began talking about so much money?

She had suspected that her marriage to Weldon would cement any business deal the two of them had made, but hadn't taken into consideration that it would increase her uncle's portion. If that was not the case, there would have been no plans to substitute one sister for the other if need be.

Glancing at the clock on the mantle, she saw that time was running short before the train would pull in. Weldon hadn't worried about her hearing that part of his plans because everything was going smoothly, and truthfully, it all seemed quite above board. It still did, which was why she had problems thinking that he would kill Simon. What could the poor railroad manager possibly do to thwart Weldon's plans? The man was only moving cattle.

She nearly grinned at that thought despite the gravity of the situation. Simon was many things, but in need of pity was not one of them!

She watched the hand on the clock move; surely her uncle and Weldon would be gone by now. She opened the door the slightest bit and looked down the hall toward Weldon's office. It appeared empty. She stepped to the other side of the door and looked in the opposite direction; all looked quiet there. Making up her mind, and a plan at the same time, Kirsten left the room, leaving the door ajar. After all, Weldon had made it a point to say that she was not a prisoner here. Now was time to act on those freedoms.

When she arrived at the parlor, it was to find that it was empty. Silas, the butler, came scurrying up to greet her.

"Can you tell me where Mr. Weldon is?" She flashed him a bright smile.

"He and Mr. Bentzer had business to attend to. I'm sure they will be back shortly."

So did she. Smiling her thanks, she headed for the smaller parlor—one Weldon assured her would be her very own after they were married. As if that was going to happen!

The advantage to the small parlor, which Weldon delightedly pointed out, was that there was a side door that led either to the basement or outdoors. She knew exactly where she was headed. The fact that the train was to make a special stop was no secret in the area. The whole town knew of it. Only certain people knew that Simon was to actually be there too, although a lot of people knew that he was working for Weldon.

She stopped, her hand on the knob of the door leading outside. What if he really was Weldon's man? She was so sure that he was not that she hadn't considered any other possibilities. Still, she couldn't let him be killed without trying to stop it. She had to warn him. Whether or not Weldon was convinced that Simon would be with him tonight didn't matter. She couldn't take the risk. She was going to have to stop Simon from reaching his destination.

With new resolve, she opened the door as quietly as possible, and slipped down the stairs along side the house, careful to stay in the shadows. If she was really lucky, she would actually get a horse from the stable without too much effort.

"What do you need, Miss Bentzer? Did you lose something?"

"No, no," she said, hoping she didn't appear as nervous as she felt. "I wanted to get a horse."

The groom stepped closer. "A horse? Now? I don't know that I can do that, Miss Bentzer. Mr. Weldon would have my hide if you was to leave the property."

"Well, that's no problem," she assured him truthfully. "I have no intention of leaving his property tonight." She leaned forward and spoke conspiringly. "See, he asked me to go down to the train with him tonight, but I was feeling poorly so I said no. But now I feel so much better that I think I should surprise him." She stepped back, watching the groom's expressive face. Finally, he shook his head.

"I'm glad you're feeling better, Miss Kirsten, but my orders come from Mr. Weldon, and he thinks you should stay right here."

Nodding her thanks, she headed back to the house, requested a cup of coffee and considered how long she would have to wait before slipping out. The sooner she left, the better. She paced, waiting for the coffee. It wasn't something she wanted, but it would prove she had returned to the house should the employees talk.

౽ ౽ ౽

Having studied the maps earlier, as well as now being more familiar with the ranch, Luke and Simon rode up from the back side, hoping to avoid as many of Weldon's men as possible.

Staring into the darkness, Simon could just make out the hastily erected fence. This was where they had spotted the men the other night. If the stampede happened here, it would almost have to be after the fact. Simon peered through the darkness. As far as he could tell, there were few cattle about—not enough to do much damage. Either they had scratched the plan or the transfer would be later than they anticipated if more cattle were being brought in. He wondered if that was the ploy Weldon was going to use tonight and, if so, when. He tensed at the sound of a voice, then relaxed slightly when Luke spoke.

"The thing that worries me is that, if we're both here, who's going to take care of identifying the printing press?"

Simon shrugged, then realized his friend might miss the action in the dark. "We know where it is; the plates have to be with them."

"What if they're not? You know that wouldn't be the first time."

Simon did know that. "Let's just hope Bentzer can tell us. If not, I think that Kirsten will have a pretty good idea."

"You think she's involved?" Luke's voice was sharp.

"Not at all," Simon said easily, "but you know I won't discount any possibility until it's over. That's not what I meant though. She seems to know that there is another press, where it is, and that there is special paper for it. How much more do I need her to tell me, other than the location of the plates? If she knows, I'm sure she'll tell us."

"*If* she knows." There was no trouble in hearing his emphasis even in the whispered conversation.

Simon knew he was taking a risk in being here tonight instead of going directly to search for the plates, but after all the trouble he had gone through to make arrangements for this special stop and getting out of jail, he wasn't exactly in a delighted mood. Weldon had put a lot of thought and effort into getting him out of the way. He must really believe that the railroad manager had very limited usefulness, Simon thought.

Luke put up a warning hand, and Simon instantly stopped. He listened intently for the sound of cattle, but heard none. Finally, he detected the low murmur of voices not wanting to be heard.

"There's someone up ahead. I can make out two figures, but can't tell if there's more," Luke said in a whisper.

Simon slid off his horse and tossed the reins to Luke as he passed him and inched closer to the men, careful to stay behind the bushes.

"There are only two," he said when he returned, and he vaulted back into his saddle, "and one of them is the sheriff."

"Interesting. Whose side do you think he's on?"

"Good question. It may come to 'killing them all and letting God sort them out.'"

Luke chuckled at the mercenary phrase. "Let's hope not." He pointed to a stand of trees behind the sheriff and the other rider, then turned his horse in that direction. From that vantage point, he could not only see the two men, but also had a clear view of the railroad track.

Giving his partner a two finger salute, Simon turned his horse and headed toward the meeting spot that he and Weldon had agreed on the other day. He could barely make out where Luke was hiding, and he knew where to look; that was good. He hoped Luke would be able to clearly keep tabs on him using the spyglass.

Turning his horse about, he dismounted and tethered the animal to a nearby tree. Stealthily, he made his way to the exact meeting spot, keeping an eye on the two men. He felt prickles run up his spine when he heard the lowing of cattle. He hoped they were further away than the newly erected fence line. The good point was that he knew, even if the cattle were intended for him, they wouldn't be let loose with Weldon in the vicinity.

ᄅ ᄅ ᄅ

Luke made himself more comfortable, resting his arm with the spyglass in his hand against the tree. If he was going to be here for any length of time, he wanted it to stay steady. He couldn't afford to miss anything. Then, he heard the sound of someone running coming from behind him. Instantly, he closed the glass and slipped it into his pocket and stepped further into the shadows of the trees. Whoever was coming through was running as quickly as they could, and they didn't seem to care much about the noise they were making.

He frowned at that. That indicated someone must be fleeing, but from whom or what? The sound was coming rapidly closer and now he could actually hear the panting breaths that accompanied the exertion. When the footfalls could be no more than seconds away, he prepared himself to pounce. He could now see it was a woman, but not make out more than her form. Kirsten? Was she running to or from Weldon?

Stepping out so that he would be on the side of the path, he startled her enough that she started to scream.

Immediately, Luke covered her mouth with his hand and grabbed her around the waist, pinning both of her arms to her sides. She tried to kick him so he widened his stance. "Shhh…" he whispered in her ear. "It's Luke. Stop screaming."

She stopped and he felt her relax somewhat, but she still held herself stiffly. He eased his hold on her mouth so that she could turn her head. "I'm going to let you go, but please just stop for a moment. Okay?"

She gave a hesitant nod, and he uncovered her mouth and stepped away from her. He kept one of his hands on a firm grip on her arm.

"What are you doing out here?" she hissed.

"My question exactly."

"I asked first."

"So you did, but I don't plan on answering first." She set her jaw at a stubborn angle, and Luke nearly laughed. It reminded him of Simon. "You were the one running, so suppose you tell me where the fire is?"

She looked at him, puzzled.

"It must be something mighty important for you to be running through the fields and woods at night." Granted, it was a track as such and they actually were not in the pastures, but they might as well be the way it smelled!

Kirsten bit her lip and turned away from him, evidently

not sure if she wanted to tell him.

"Listen, Kirsten, you can trust me."

She gave him a mocking laugh. "Weldon said that too, and—" She abruptly ended the thought.

"And what?"

"Never mind. It's not important."

Tugging on her arm, Luke spun her to face him. He had a feeling it was very important. "If it's the reason you're running, then you better tell me right now." She stared at him, but didn't answer. Taking a deep breath, he asked if had anything to co with Weldon's plan for tonight.

She started at that. "You know that he's planning to kill Simon?"

Luke shook his head. "I was referring to the train delivery, but I have a feeling it's one and the same." That the man would stoop to murder didn't surprise him in the least. "Did he say how or when?"

Shaking her head again, she told him the little she overheard. "I thought if I could get closer, tell Simon what Weldon and my uncle are planning, he would be able to save himself."

Just then, they both heard the sound of a wagon coming from another direction, but converging at the point where Simon was to have been.

"You're not going anywhere, now," Luke said. "It's too late." He only hoped that it wasn't too late for his friend. Pulling the spyglass from his pocket, he looked around and saw that Simon was still in the shadows. The sheriff had moved in to the group, but from the distance, it was still unclear as to which side he was on.

She put her fist to her mouth as if to silence herself. He understood the feeling. Even as he heard Kirsten's near silent sobs, he tuned them out. She didn't know what Simon was capable of.

They could hear the train clicking its way down the track, slowing for the scheduled pick-up. As it slid to a stop, the steam billowing from its stack as if impatient to be going, Simon moved out from the trees.

By now, Weldon and Bentzer had taken the wagon as close to the track as possible and started to unload the lead box from the wagon bed. Even from the distance, Luke could see that it took both of them to move it.

♩ ♩ ♩

Simon watched, still waiting for the sheriff to make a move one way or another. He hated to accuse the man falsely.

"All in order?" the sheriff asked as he dismounted. Simon watched as the man ground tied his horse and walked closer to the box now on the ground. The other man with him did the same. Another deputy? Simon didn't see a badge, but had no idea of the man's identity.

"Looks good. Twenty-five thousand dollars in new greenbacks heading to the U.S. Treasury. Doesn't get better than that."

That was more than Simon needed to hear.

"Where did you leave Simon Barr?" Weldon turned to direct his question to the sheriff.

"Right here," Simon said as he stepped out from behind his cover.

He had the pleasure of watching all four men whip around in surprise, hands reaching for their guns. He already had his drawn and pointing at them.

"Now listen here, Mr. Barr. If you're thinking of running off with this money, you best think again. The sheriff here is not only the law in these parts, he's the best shot in the area."

"Hands way up," Simon said in a conversational tone. "Now, I want to make something clear," he said when they complied after looking at one another. "First, I am very interested in the money in that chest." As soon as Weldon started to let his hand droop, Simon shook his head. "Tsk, tsk, Weldon. I said hands up." He used his gunpoint to motion the man should raise his hands.

"I believe I'm interested for a reason different than what you anticipate." Seeing that he had their attention, he continued. "Allow me to formally introduce myself. My name is Simon Barr, of the Secret Service."

"What is that?" the sheriff asked.

"You surprise me, sheriff. It means that I am a federal law officer, and, as such, I place all of you under arrest."

The sheriff chuckled. "What are you talkin' about?"

"You arrest *him*, sheriff," Weldon said.

"You may certainly try," Simon said, "but I assure you, I am who I say. I answer to the Director of the U.S. Treasury and President Grant."

From the corner of his eye, Simon saw Weldon reach for his gun. Before the man even touched the butt of his gun in its sheath strapped to his leg, Simon spun and fired a shot in his direction, then immediately turned back to the other three. He didn't have to see if he hit target—the top of Weldon's gun. He could hear from the man's yelp of surprise that he had.

"Now I want to see what exactly is in that chest." Using his free hand, he motioned for Weldon to come closer. "Open it," he demanded.

When the man refused to comply, Simon reached out and backhanded him across the mouth. The other three started to move in, but Simon held his ground, although he did send a piercing whistle into the night air.

Instantly, there were three shots fired in succession. The men looked around them in surprise. And even more so when the doors of the train slid open and over a dozen federal cavalry men poured out, immediately surrounding them.

The sheriff reached for his gun, but seeing Simon turn his attention to him, he immediately released it.

"Very good," Simon told him. "Remember, hands way up." Once they were in the air again, the federal troops went around to the four men, removing weapons from their holsters, then frisking them.

"They're clean, sir," the man in charge of the troops addressed Simon.

"I demand to know the meaning of this," the sheriff said.

"And I believe that I explained it quite clearly," Simon said. "You're all under arrest. You'll be taken to Washington and tried for counterfeiting."

"Counterfeiting?" Weldon let he word burst from his lips. "Are you insare, man?"

"Not to my knowledge," Simon replied as he watched the troops tie the men's hands behind their backs.

"I own a bank! I would never be involved in something as underhanded—"

"Open the chest," Simon demanded.

When the man stood in silence, Simon nodded to one of the nearby soldiers who correctly interpreted that as a signal to shoot the lock off.

"Now, bring me a bundle of those bills, please." Simon requested.

The man complied. Sheathing his gun, Simon fanned the bills. The truth was that, without a light, he couldn't see anything. And he had no intention of lighting a fire with only one eye on the group in front of him—even with federal soldiers at the ready.

He called one of the soldiers over and told him to fetch a lantern. In the mean time, he held the bills in his hand and watched the men in front of him sweat. With part of his mind, he wondered where Luke was. He had expected him when he let out the whistle.

He didn't have long to wait. Before the soldier returned with the lantern, Luke had made his way to his side, but not alone. He looked around his partner. "Kirsten." He kept the surprise from his voice. And why was she with Luke? He shot a glance at his partner, then tilted his head in the direction of the four men, one of whom was her uncle.

"Kirsten!" her uncle called out. "What in the hell have you got mixed up in now?"

"Me?"

"Leave her out of this," Simon growled. He must have been more menacing than he thought because Luke stepped closer to him. *To pull him back?*

Her uncle gave a laugh that set Simon's hair on edge. It must have done the same for Luke because now he actually took a step in front of Simon, and, this time, he didn't think it was to restrain him.

"She's the one who bought the paper."

"Shut up, you fool," Weldon hissed the words at him.

Simon and Luke looked at each other and grinned. Even without the light, Simon knew they had just confessed to counterfeiting. Whether or not the bills in the chest were counterfeit, he would know in a minute.

The sergeant came back bearing a lantern, which he held above Simon's shoulder so that he could examine the bills.

Like the other bills he had seen, these were excellent forgeries; nearly impossible to distinguish from the real ones. As Simon started to compare the serial numbers, his heart nearly sank. The first three serial numbers were different! Then, he looked more closely. There were only three serial numbers in the stack. He called for another stack and tossed the first one to Luke. He looked through them once, then again, then let out a low whistle.

"I must compliment you, Weldon," Simon said. "These are among the best, but counterfeit nonetheless."

"Don't be ridiculous. Of course they're genuine. Why else would I send them to the Treasury?"

"A very good question," Luke said, "but one I would wait to answer if I were you."

"And just who are you? A store keeper?" Weldon snorted.

"Actually, gentlemen, this is my esteemed partner, Luke Hayden."

"Partner in what? That's what I would like to know," the sheriff said.

"It seems you're hearing is not so good," Simon said. "Me"—he pointed to himself and then to Luke—"and my partner are both secret service agents for the federal government."

"Do you think I believe that story?"

Simon cocked his head in the direction of the train, and addressed the sergeant. "You can take them now. Major Trent will be waiting for them in Washington."

"Kirsten," her uncle called. "You better confess to your part before they try to hoodwink you too."

"Sergeant!" Simon caught the man's attention, and then walked up to meet Mr. Bentzer. "You may take the others," he told the troops. "Give me a minute here."

Except for two soldiers standing nearby, everyone else boarded the train. Simon looked around her uncle toward the soldiers. "Make sure the box is secure, and then you can come back for your prisoner." He could hardly tell them that he had unfinished business with the man.

They did as he requested.

"I'm not a prisoner yet, Mr. Barr."

"Well, you are under arrest, and caught with a group of counterfeiters. All in good time, Bentzer. However, that's not what I want to talk to you about."

The man straightened and chuckled. "Think I don't know the way you've been sniffing around my niece—"

Simon backhanded him without saying a word. When he did speak, his words were measured and precise. "I intend to find out exactly what role your niece has played in this operation, but I assure you, if I find that you have lied or placed more blame on her than there should be, I will come after you."

The man didn't say a word.

Simon's voice dropped another notch and he leaned closer. "You do understand?"

Both soldiers were at his side before the man could say anything, and he didn't. Simon watched until they were on board the train, and the train started back down the track.

Leaving Kirsten, Luke walked down to meet him. "You know, I would like to take another look at that machine and whatever plates they were using. Those bills were quite good."

Simon whipped his head around to look at him, then burst out laughing. "Thinking of going into business?"

Luke scoffed, and pushed the bills that he still held into the pocket of his coat. "I'm heading back to town. Do you want me to take your horse?"

"No, no. I'll need him to get back myself. I'm going to take the wagon back to Weldon's. Pride can be tied on the back."

"And Kirsten?"

Glancing over to where she was still standing, staring at nothing, Simon said, "She'll come with me."

$$ ₹ ₹ ₹ $$

She hardly said a word on her way back to the ranch. Once there, Simon requested a mount for her. While it was being readied, he had the housekeeper get Kirsten some coffee. She looked as if she were in shock— because of his role or that of the men in her life until now, he had no way of knowing. He wanted to offer comfort, but there were still several things he had to do; the first, informing the foreman that he was in charge for the time being.

Then there was the bank. He nearly groaned at that thought. Before the bank even opened, he and Luke were going to have to go through all of the bills. They had seen them earlier, but hadn't known exactly what they were looking for. Now they did. He refused to think of that at the moment.

"Weldon and a few others had to leave unexpectedly," he told the foreman. "For the moment, you're in charge. You know how things are supposed to run. If you have any problems, contact me."

The foreman raised his eyebrows in surprise. "When will Mr. Weldon be back?"

"Not for some time, but I'm sure we'll know better what direction to take shortly. But for now, this would be best." Frankly, Simon wouldn't blame them if they all left. As soon as they found out that most of their pay and bonuses had been bogus money—well, Weldon should be glad that he was, or would be, behind bars.

Once the mount was brought around, he went up the steps to the house and called the housekeeper. Briefly, he told her much the same thing that he had told the foreman. Kirsten still sat in the kitchen. She looked as if she hadn't touched her coffee. Simon couldn't say that he cared for her vacant stare, it made him tremendously uncomfortable.

She didn't say anything when he leaned over her and put his hand on her shoulder, asking if she were ready to leave. She simply pushed the chair out and stood. She allowed him to help her to mount, but didn't do much else. Concerned about her state of mind, there was still little he could do, especially on Weldon's property. Vaulting on to the back of his own horse, he leaned next to her and took the reins from her unresisting hands and led her horse. He hoped she would stay on. They didn't even make it down the drive when it was apparent t was going to be a long ride this way. Sighing, Simon stopped on the other side of the property gates and dismounted.

Reaching up, he grasped her by the waist. That was the first reaction he had from her and it wasn't favorable. Her eyes widened in fright, and rather than use his shoulders for support, she pushed away from him. He tightened his grip, and spoke in a soothing tone. "Kirsten, you have to leave here."

She nodded once, and she no longer pushed against him. Simon frowned. It was as if she was a rag doll, completely lifeless. Now her hands merely rested on his shoulders. Rather than put her down, he carried her over to his horse and lifted her so that she would sit in front of him. He hoped she stayed on until he mounted. He would not call one of the other men to help. Right now, they just stood around watching. He supposed they had their own reasons, but he knew the longer he stayed, the longer they speculated, the greater the danger to himself and to her.

Once he was in the saddle, he picked up the reins, his arms encircling her. She sat straight. Not that he blamed her. Picking up the reins of her horse, he turned it in the direction of the barn and smacked his flank, sending him back to the stables. Then, he walked his horse to the road. When he finally broke into a canter, she did lean against him. He suspected it was more from exhaustion than anything else.

The ride back to town was all too short as far as he was concerned. He tried not to let his arms tighten about her, but there was no denying that he liked the way she felt there. She felt right. In flicking the reins, he inadvertently brushed his arm across her breast. He bit back the groan he could feel forming in his throat. There was no sense in speculating what she thought; he already knew that. After all, he was the one who had just arrested her fiancé and her uncle. That would be enough reason for her to hate him, even if she had said she had no feelings for either man.

If that was not enough, he *still* didn't know if she was involved in their scheme. It tore at his insides to think that she might be, but he was experienced enough to know that it was very possible, and in all likelihood, probable.

She let her head fall against his chest, and he deeply inhaled the scent of her. And promptly wished he hadn't. He was always going to think of her when he smelled lemons.

For now, the question was where to take her where she would be safe. He really didn't believe that her uncle or Weldon would do anything, or more accurately, *could* do anything from where they were, but it was still something to consider. Staying with him would not be the best thing. He wasn't certain that Weldon's men wouldn't show up some time during the night. He almost relished the thought, but not if he had to worry about Kirsten too.

₴ ₴ ₴

Kirsten struggled to come out of the fog that had enveloped her since she'd first run into Luke in the woods. It seemed a lot longer ago than a few hours. It had been a little embarrassing to think that she couldn't even seat a horse, but the alternative—being wrapped in Simon's arms, even in so impersonal a manner—was preferable.

When her head felt too heavy to hold upright, she let it fall against his chest. It was strong and solid. She loved hearing the steady thump of his heart. From the warmth of her body next to his she could smell horse and man and leather. It was a comforting scent and she let her eyes drift close. Then, they snapped open. *Where was she going to spend the night?* She asked the question tentatively.

"I was thinking the same thing. Here are the options and you tell me which is best for you." He suggested her uncle's house, and a shudder ran through her. "Or perhaps we can make arrangements for you to stay at Kate's tonight. I'm sure she would take you in."

In a brothel? That was safe? "Can't I stay behind Doc's or in the hotel with you?" It cost a lot for her to say those words.

"No, you can't."

She bit her lip. He offered no explanation, but then, none was needed, she reasoned. After all, if what he had said back at the ranch was true, he was the law. There was no way that he could believe she wasn't guilty. Not that she was exactly sure of what he suspected she was guilty of.

She licked her lips, but didn't get a chance to utter a word. They were in the middle of town now. It was full dark and rather quiet except for the sounds coming from the saloon. He reined his horse in front of Doc's, and she breathed a sigh of relief. He slipped from the saddle, but instructed her to stay mounted for the moment.

Simon reached out a fist and thumped firmly on the door. It was answered promptly by the doctor.

"What can—" He broke off what he started to say and headed toward the horse. "Miss Kirsten, are you hurt?"

Simon arrived before the doctor and it was his hands that lifted her from the saddle. She looked down as she brushed her skirt so that he wouldn't notice the heat in her cheeks, if he could see in the dark. Frankly, after the incident at the ranch when he checked the bills, she couldn't be sure that he didn't have cat eyes.

She closed her own eyes when she felt his strong hands on her waist. She didn't want him to release her. To her surprise, he didn't immediately do so. He kept one arm around her waist as they followed the doctor in.

"Do you think you can get her some coffee and food?" Simon asked as soon as the door closed behind them.

"Certainly. Come this way." He led them to the kitchen, put on the coffee and excused himself to find his wife. They were back in a moment, only long enough for Simon to see that Kirsten was seated.

"Care to tell me what's going on?" the doctor said as he pulled mugs from the shelf and his wife started slicing bread to use for sandwiches.

Simon gave her a chance to explain, but she remained silent. After all, what was there to say?

"First, Kirsten needs a safe place to stay tonight. And I do mean safe."

The doctor raised his eyebrows and stared at her. "What happened?"

Simon chuckled. "I'm afraid that sounded more dramatic than it need be. The truth is, she has nowhere else to stay that won't damage her reputation and she needs to be where someone will be able to care for her. If nothing else, I know that I can count on you to be sure she doesn't go into shock." He pointed to the food in front of her. "Which is why I asked she be given food and drink."

"Shouldn't Weldon take care of this? In fact, I thought I heard that you were at his ranch," the doctor said, studying her.

She couldn't resist the involuntary shudder at the other man's name. "Weldon is nothing to me," she said. She saw Simon's speculative glance. "He's not! Why do you think I was there tonight?"

"That remains to be seen." Simon pushed himself away from the table. He reached his hand out, as if he would touch her, but then let it drop to his side.

"Are you really a secret service agent?"

The doctor and his wife looked on in surprise.

Simon looked at them, gave them a crooked smile, and introduced himself to them.

"I never heard of such a thing," the doctor said.

"I assure you, it's quite true," Simon responded. "My partner and I were here to do a job, and we've nearly finished." Kirsten turned her head away when he looked in her direction.

"Your partner?" the doctor asked.

"Luke Hayden."

The doctor's wife gasped. "You mean that nice store keeper is really working with you? He's a lawman?"

"'Fraid so, ma'am."

"Who will run the store?"

Simon chuckled. "I'm sure the town will find someone."

"Just where was the sheriff while all this was going on? Did he know you were a law man?"

"He does now," Simon said.

Kirsten's voice was low, wooden. "He arrested all of them—the sheriff, Weldon, some of the hands, and my uncle."

The doctor groped for a chair. "What?"

Simon excused himself. "I'm sure Kirsten can fill you in on the details, but for now, I do have to get back to my duties."

Chapter Eleven

No matter how distasteful duties were, they had to be tended to. Simon ran his hand through his hair in frustration. He wanted Kristen to be innocent, but he couldn't trust his own judgment. For that reason alone he was glad to find Luke waiting for him at the hotel. One thing about Luke, Simon never worried if he had a key or not! He was seated in the comfortable chair in the room, watching the door.

"Took you long enough," he greeted him.

Simon unbuckled his gun belt and laid it on the dresser. "I couldn't leave Kirsten at Weldon's," he said as he sat on the edge of the bed.

"True. Since I don't see her here, where did you leave her? Her uncle's house?"

"Couldn't do that either. Aside from the fact that she shouldn't be alone, she was in shock, Luke. Her uncle may have evidence there. We need to check."

"You don't—" Luke waved his hand and the thought away. "You don't think she's involved, do you?" he asked when Simon made no comment.

"You asked that before. I want to believe differently, but do you have any idea how she could not be?"

"Well, yes, quite a few, actually." Luke stood and started pacing. "Did you know that she was out there tonight to warn *you*?"

That caught his attention. "About what?"

"That Weldon and her uncle were planning to kill you."

"Does that surprise you?"

"Not me," Luke stated, "but it rather took her by surprise."

It was something he was going to have to think on. And the fact that Luke could vouch for her was definitely in her favor, and h s if he was honest. Standing, he walked to the window and peered out to the street.

"Think someone followed you?"

"Not really." Being cautious was part of his nature in spite of what Luke often thought. "I would be surprised if they had." He dropped the edge of the curtain he was holding and turned to lean against the dresser, careful to stay out of view of the window. His longevity in the business wasn't all due to luck. "I think we should head over to that house tonight. It won't be long before someone hears the men are on their way to prison."

"True. I don't think anyone in town would know just yet, but Weldon's men have to know something went on. And we have no idea how many of them, if any, were involved."

Nodding agreement, Simon reached for his gun belt and refastened it. He had planned to wait until morning, which wasn't that far off, but knowing that he wouldn't sleep for thinking of Kirsten, it was probably best to keep busy.

It didn't take long to search the house, and find that there was nothing out of the ordinary there. Rifling through the small stack of papers on the desk brought nothing to light. Most were bills, indicating that her uncle did most of his bookwork at home. There was an unsealed note addressed to Kirsten. Simon held it for a moment before opening it. This was the same as any other case, he reminded himself. It was from Maj. He quickly skimmed it and put it back in place.

Simon hadn't expected there would be anything, but had hoped for a few of the counterfeit bills. If they were in the house, they weren't in any likely spots. He couldn't bring himself to go through Kirsten's room. What if he did find evidence there? Would he be strong enough to turn it over? It disturbed him that he couldn't even trust himself, so he insisted Luke do it while he checked the uncle's room.

"Nothing," Luke said when they met at the top of the landing.

Simon expelled a breath he hadn't even realized he had been holding. He allowed himself the smallest of smiles, but knew she wasn't in the clear yet. Her uncle had mentioned something about ordering paper. "I'm satisfied that there is nothing here."

"I agree," Luke said. "I think the most likely place would be the newspaper office."

Nodding, Simon started down the stairs. He hadn't thought there would be anything here, but he had wanted to be certain.

The newspaper office was a short walk from the house. With the growing light, the men were careful to keep to the shadows. Checking for an open door, they found they were all locked. In a matter of seconds, Luke had them inside.

Listening to make sure no one else was about, and to get a feel for the sounds of the building, they stood quietly.

Striking a match, Simon held it in front of him, trying to see where there might be lamps. Identifying one, he shook the match out and made his way to a desk. Lighting another match, he, in turn, lit the lamp and turned the wick low. Picking it up, they made their way about the office. It was much like any other newspaper office. Another smaller desk—a reporter's desk?—held a sharpened pencil and paper at the ready.

Finding another lamp, Simon stopped to light it and handed one to Luke. They made their way easily to the press room. The modern press was certainly an improvement over some of the antiquated ones Simon had seen. He ran his finger over the platen, picking up a slight ink residue. He looked at his finger under the light. In the dim lighting it was difficult to tell if it was really black or green.

Simon cocked his head toward a door. "I'm guessing what we're looking for is going to be found behind locked doors." Only it wasn't in this one. Careful not to upset trays of type or bottles of ink, they weren't so conscientious of boxes of rags, pencils or tablets.

Resting his hand on one of the boxes, Simon sighed in frustration. "Those plates have to be here somewhere. In fact..." He started looking around the floor, then stopped where he started.

"In fact, what?"

"Kirsten said there was a cellar. It has to be under this box. There is no other opening. Help me move this." Setting their lamps down, the men moved the box holding the type.

Before they had completely moved it, Simon tapped the floorboards with his foot and smiled. "It's here," he said in response to the hollow sound. "Let's get this out of the way." With renewed effort, they managed to push the chest clear of the trap door.

Standing to the side, Simon lifted the ring and pulled. It came up on well-oiled hinges, which made the men grin again.

"If that press isn't down there, there's something else they don't want us to find," Luke said.

Simon rapidly made his way down the steps. Lighting another match, he made out sconces against the wall. He had two of them lit before Luke joined him. They both looked around. This section was kept as neat, if not more so, than the pressroom.

In the corner of the room, there was a small workbench. Simon headed there, removing the cloth lying over something. He gave out a low whistle of surprise, which Luke echoed as soon as he arrived.

"There has to be an easy forty thousand there," Luke said.

Simon rifled through the edge of the stacks of bills, determining if they were all the same denomination—they were. "With this many stacks of twenties, there has to be at least that amount."

Luke moved to another cloth-covered pile and pushed away the covering. There were several piles of fifty-dollar bills. Smaller than the number of twenties, but still significant. After they uncovered all of the piles around, they still hadn't discovered the plates, not that they expected it to be easy. Usually, the plates were very well hidden. After emptying drawers and trays, they weren't much wiser.

"These bills look pretty fresh," Luke said. "It's very possible those plates are under our very nose."

"They're fresh all right," Simon said, holding up his finger with the ink stain. "You know, I bet they are in plain sight." Grinning, he made his way back up the stairs into the pressroom. He hadn't expected to find them here, and he hadn't. Now he went over to desk and looked around again. He was thumping the wall and the desk when Luke joined him.

"They're here," Simon insisted. "I can feel it. They're right under—" He stopped mid-sentence and stomped his foot near the desk, then did it again in strategic spots. He got on one side of the desk and called Luke to help him slide it away from the wall. This time, when he stomped, both men smiled at the hollow sound.

Reaching into his jacket for his knife, Simon pried a few boards loose and was able to detect a small safe. Simon put his hand in and withdrew the small Lily safe. "Your turn," he said to Luke, and shifted out of the way.

"Well, you can't have all the fun," Luke said as he knelt on the floor next to the safe. Leaning his ear close to the tumbler, he worked to get the correct combination. Once it was open, Simon reached for the lamp they had left on the desk and brought it closer.

Removing the wrapping from the rectangular package, the men laid the plates on the table and looked to make sure they were correct. Simon removed the bills he had brought with him from the bank, and from Weldon's ranch. After lining up the fronts and backs of the bills, Simon leaned forward and picked up one of the front plates, holding it even closer to the light.

"What did you find?" Luke asked, leaning over his partner's shoulder.

Instead of answering him, Simon wrapped the plates again. He shoved two in his jacket and indicated that Luke should do the same, then he reached inside the safe again, sliding his hand around. He stopped when he encountered another piece of cloth, and he gave a satisfied grunt. He shoved that package into his pocket without looking, closed and locked the safe and stuck it back under the floorboards.

"Help me move the desk back in place," he told Luke.

When they were finished, Luke said, "Mind telling me what that was all about?"

"Not just yet. Right now, we need to get a handful of bills, a few from each stack."

"You have a reason for this, right?" Luke asked even as he headed toward the stairs. Once down there, the men quickly gathered some bills, covered the stacks and extinguished the sconces.

It wasn't until they were back at the mercantile that Simon told him of his suspicions. First, he took out the two front plates from his jacket, unwrapped them and laid them on the table for Luke's inspection. "Anything look odd to you?"

Luke studied them for several moments, one then the other, and then in comparison. He started to shake his head, then stopped. "The serial numbers are short!"

"Are they?" Again, Simon reached into his jacket and, this time, withdrew the bills they had taken. He spread them out in his hand before laying them on the table. "Now, these are not mine, correct? Not from the Treasury," he clarified.

Luke nodded with a puzzled frown. "I don't see what you're getting at, Sime. I know they're counterfeit; I saw you pick them up."

Simon laid the bills on the table as he continued to speak. "And what's the one thing all counterfeit bills have in common?"

"The same serial number," Luke said without hesitation. His tone implied that Simon was daft for asking. Then he came to lean over the table near Simon. He looked through a few of the bills. "But these have different numbers."

"Ah! Only some are different." Simon spread the rest of the bills in his hand and started to sort them into piles according to serial numbers. There were three different numbers.

"Amazing!" Luke walked back over to the plates with the three different bills in his hand. Studying one of the plates, he used the edge of the bill to point to the slot. "I wondered why there were only three numbers. This little slot makes them interchangeable! But who would go through so much trouble? Most counterfeiters don't."

That was true. Simon grabbed one of the kitchen chairs, turned it about and straddled it. "These are extraordinary counterfeiters, Luke. Remember, they wanted to ship this to the U.S. Treasury. They had to be extra careful. Mixed in with the genuine currency at the bank, no one would question it. It's unlikely anyone would notice."

"Do you think they stopped at three sets?"

Simon ran his hand around the back of his neck and rubbed. "That's the problem. I don't know. And who knows if the men will tell us everything. As I see it, we need to contact Washington and see what they're suggestions are."

Luke laid everything on the table before opening the door that led to the store and the telegraph. Leaving the door ajar gave him enough light to make his way to the machine.

Bracing himself on one hand, he used the other to send a code, making sure someone was on the other end. In a moment, he had a response and proceeded to send his coded message through. Normally, on a dedicated wire, the code wasn't necessary.

When he finished, he left the door ajar and joined Simon who was making a pot of coffee.

"It'll be a while before they get back to us. I'd be surprised if it was before morning."

Simon cocked his head to the window. "Sunrise in less than two hours, so I daresay you're right."

"One of us, if not both, will probably have to go to Washington."

Simon shrugged. "That's typical."

"I don't know if I'm ready," Luke admitted.

"Maj?" Simon reached for two mugs and poured the coffee, then handed one to his partner.

Luke took a sip before answering. "I'd like to see her again before we go back or move to the next assignment."

"Not a problem, I can go," Simon said, "but you're going to have to find her first." His going to Washington would be a big problem for him personally, but he would never admit that to Luke. It wasn't often the man asked anything for himself.

Simon wanted to talk with Kirsten before he left, but then again, he wasn't sure that would be the best thing in his current state of mind. Right now he still had a job to do and he intended to see it finished. There would be no problem with only one of them traveling. Except it turned out that the Major wanted both of them.

ㄹ ㄹ ㄹ

The sun was high before Kirsten awoke the next morning. She felt drained of energy, but closer to being herself than she had been the night before. She didn't hurry to dress, but instead sat on the bed thinking over the events.

The doctor and his wife had been very understanding, and offered good advice. Now that her uncle was no longer in the picture, Maj would not have to stay away. The two of them could set up housekeeping. Her biggest decision would be if she should stay in town and take over her uncle's newspaper and printing business—the legitimate one, she reminded herself bitterly—or if she should look to work for one of the larger newspapers around the area. That would mean moving.

She wished she could have talked to Simon, then gave a travesty of a smile. She meant the Simon she thought he was, not the secret service agent who made believe that he was friends with her and others. She closed her eyes for a moment, remembering the few encounters Maj had with Luke. Her sister would be heartbroken if she ever found out. She refused to say "too." She wasn't certain, but if Luke was an agent, the same as Simon, she wondered if that meant he would move on. The mercantile here might keep him anchored for only a short while.

Taking a deep breath, she stood with new resolve. That made it simple in a way. She would have to leave. Now, with a purpose, her movements were much more efficient and confident. She slowed, remembering that she still didn't know where Maj was so her sister could hardly fall in with her plans. Washing her face, she donned her clothes that the doctor's wife had pressed for her and headed downstairs.

Eleanor, the doctor's wife, looked at her sharply when she entered the kitchen. "There are still shadows under your eyes, but you look much better, dear." She steered Kirsten toward the kitchen. "Let me get you some breakfast."

"I really can't," she insisted. "It's not that I don't appreciate your hospitality, because I do, but I have to find my sister. We have to make some decisions, and the sooner we do that, the better."

"I understand. Start your search, but plan to come back here tonight." Seeing that Kirsten was already shaking her head, the doctor's wife smiled, "Just come for dinner then. No matter what you do, you won't want to start out tired and on an empty stomach."

Thanking her, Kirsten made her way to the brothel where Maj had stayed. She had hoped that Kate could give her some piece of information, no matter how small.

"I have no idea where she went," the head housekeeper said. "She slipped out sometime after dinner the other night and I haven't seen her since." The woman was positively indignant. "And I'll see that she doesn't get this week's wages!"

The other night. That had to be the night they'd stayed in Doc's backroom. It seemed a lifetime ago now.

"Her case is gone and whatever clothes she had here." She wagged her finger in front of Kirsten's face. "If she comes back here beggin' for a job, she'll not get one, even if it's layin' on her back!"

Kirsten gasped. "That's a vile thing to say! And she won't be coming back here. I'm looking for her to tell her just that." How had Maj ever had anything nice to say about the woman?

Snorting, the housekeeper practically pushed Kirsten out of the front door, slamming it in her face.

She hurried to her uncle's house in hope that there was some word there. No one would have disturbed it, she thought, since her uncle had been tied up with Weldon and his scheme.

A note addressed to her lay on the top of the pile on the desk. She lifted it slowly, reluctant to open it. Hadn't her sister believed her when she said that she was no longer living at her uncle's?

Taking a deep breath, she opened the note, quickly skimming over the few words scribbled there. Maj was gone. She had taken the little ready money she could find and was to buy a ticket as far east as she could go.

Kirsten's problem was trying to figure out how much money her sister really had! She sat there, letter in her hand, unmoving for what seemed eons. It was difficult to marshal her thoughts into any kind of order. Finally, she began to grow stiff from being in one place too long and stood.

Now that she was here, there was no reason to go back to the doctor's, no matter what Simon thought. She nearly snorted at that thought as she made her way up the stairs. Simon was gone, what he thought didn't matter. He would never know one way or the other.

She made her plans. She would start looking for jobs at other newspapers and slowly make her way east, hoping she would find Maj along the way. It would give her the opportunity to look for her and leave word at the same time. Even if she only worked as a stringer at some of the papers, it would give her more freedom and more money to continue her search.

With new resolve, she changed her clothes and freshened

herself, preparing to go back to the mercantile—well, maybe not there, but definitely to the telegraph office. Normalville was only two day trip. She was sure she could get a job at that paper. She would wire the editor today and let him know she would be in the area.

ع ع ع

Simon and Luke were under direction to take the train to Washington. Since it would be another day before they could catch the train from Pine Grove to Washington, they decided to ride to Flatwood and catch an earlier one. It proved to be well worth their while when they found that train with the federal officers and Weldon and his cohorts were still in the area.

"There was an eight hour delay out of Pine Grove," the station master told them. "They decided to stop here for water and wood."

Delighted with another opportunity to interrogate the prisoners before seeing the Major, they wasted no time in talking to them.

"I think it's best for you to talk to Bentzer," Simon said.

"You're probably right, but I'm thinking maybe it would be better if I talked to both of them," he said wryly. "It could be said that you have a score to settle with each of them."

Simon heaved a sigh and agreed. "What about you? Are you all right talking to Bentzer?"

"Better than you."

Grunting in response, Simon had a feeling Luke was right. "I'll take care of the horses and get tickets to Washington."

They had already traveled by train through the night, and Luke couldn't seem to stop grumbling about it.

"It could be worse," Simon assured him. "We could have had to start from Denver or San Francisco."

"You're all heart, Sime. I didn't want to go to begin with."

"I know."

Luke shot Simon a questioning look at his quiet tone, but Simon turned away, studying the family across the aisle from them. Luke's words caused him to pay attention. "Look at it this way, at least something good came out of that stop."

Simon gave him a tight smile. "That's one way to look at

it. I should have believed in Kirsten earlier. There was no way she could have been involved."

"Neither of us knew that for sure. Now that we have confessions from Weldon and Bentzer, in front of federal troops, there is no going back."

"I had been meaning to ask how you managed that."

Ignoring the questions and snorting lightly, Luke repositioned his hat on his head and slouched into his seat.

"You know, it still amazes me as to what those two men could have done if they hadn't been caught."

"Remarkable," came Luke's sleepy reply. "But the bad guys are caught, the economy is safe and Kirsten is innocent." His voice trailed off toward the end, but Simon heard it, and silently agreed.

After a bit, the train slowed, and the conductor came back shouting the stop. "We're going to be here for an hour," he told everyone. "You can grab dinner or stretch your legs."

Simon was inclined to stay right where he was. He hadn't liked the way he left things with Kirsten, but when he got back, perhaps they could discuss it. He hadn't even been aware that he had planned to return. After Luke poked him in the ribs for the second time, he stood.

"I'm going to send a telegram," he said.

Luke followed him down the aisle and off the train. "To?"

"To Kirsten. I want to set up a meeting when we get back."

"Now that is a good idea, Sime. Think I'll follow you. Perhaps Kirsten has heard something of her sister."

Crossing the platform, the men headed for the telegraph office. Grabbing the pad of paper on the counter and a pencil, Simon started to write out his brief message.

"You want to send that message?" the telegrapher said, ambling over to the counter.

Simon tore off the top sheet. "That is the general idea." He smiled, taking the sting out of his words. "What will that be?" He reached for his wallet.

The man counted out the words and gave him a price.

"I have one too," Luke said. He hastily wrote his message.

"I have to take them in order, you know."

Luke chuckled. "I know, but they're going to the same place, so if you get the receiver on the line, it will make it quicker."

The man grumbled his way back to the counter and told Luke his fee, then returned to the telegraph key. Simon turned away from the counter, hiding a grin. "Pleasant fellow, isn't he?" he said under his breath.

Luke started to laugh, but hastily turned it to a cough.

Both men frowned, looked at each other and turned back to the telegrapher as they listened to the series of taps coming in.

"Hold it," Luke said.

It was the telegrapher's turn to frown. "Can't very well send the message if you're interrupting."

"You can't send it anyway," Simon said. Using his chin, he pointed to the telegraph key. "The receiver said the party is not in town."

They heard the clattering of the key again. This time, Simon interrupted. "Ask him if he knows where she went?"

"You can't do that." He came bustling over to the counter. "I'm going to have to ask you men to leave. That's private information."

"It's all right," Simon said. "We're with the United States Secret Service and we're trying to locate this woman."

"Never heard such a thing."

"He is telling the truth," Luke said.

The man still looked at him suspiciously.

Simon tore another sheet from the pad of messages and wrote out another one. "Send this first."

"Simon Barr and Luke Hayden, U.S. Treasury. Please confirm." The operator read it out loud and looked at them askance.

"It will only take a moment, but do ask the receiver to stand by first."

Once the man got the confirmation, he turned to look at the two men now in quiet conversation, and turned back to his original receiver. The answer that returned wasn't helpful. It merely stated that she was searching for her sister and heading east. Who would have thought the telegraphers would be such a chatty lot?

Thanking the man, it was a subdued duo that headed back to the train.

"Any ideas?"

Shaking his head, Simon boarded the train. As he

stepped onto the platform, he looked about, mostly from habit, and stopped. He watched the figure as she boarded the train, then turned to Luke, who had been looking for what caught his partner's attention, and slapped him on the shoulder. "That's one answer." He stepped into the car, allowing room for Simon to join him.

His heart wanted to believe it was Kirsten, but his brain said the odds were extremely unlikely. "You stay here in case she comes back this far. I'm going to go through the other cars. It could be her."

"I always said you should have been Irish with your luck!" Luke made himself comfortable in the aisle seat.

Simon didn't believe these odds were in his favor, but he owed it to himself to find out if it really was her or if his mind was playing tricks. Granted, there were only two tracks, but that she should be on *this train now* would be a stroke of good fortune.

Making his way through the crowded car, he received more than his share of disgruntled looks. He ignored them. He went through one more before he finally spotted her. She was sitting near the window. Amazingly, the seat next to her was empty.

Walking slowly now, Simon made his way to that seat and slid in. She didn't even bother to look and see who sat next to her. Shifting so that he could rest his arm on the back of the seat, he let his fingers inch slowly toward her. She must have sensed his nearness because she stiffened.

"Kirsten," he said softly.

This time, she did whip around to face him. "Simon!"

He was relieved to see the joy in her face as she said his name, then it was quickly masked.

Instantly, she looked down at her hands resting in her lap. "Have you come to arrest me now?"

"What are you talking about?" He kept his voice low and leaned in toward her. Not that he could have stopped himself. This close, he had to inhale the essence of her. "I told you I had things to tend to and then I would be back. Why did you leave?"

She jerked her head up and looked at him. "How did you find me?"

Giving her a slight smile, he said, "The sheerest luck." He reached out and played with the tendril of her hair that escaped her hat. He took it as a good sign that she didn't jerk away. The look she gave him made him want to gather her to him and not let go. He tucked her hair behind her ears and moved his hand to link his fingers together, his elbow resting on the back of the seat. He made an effective barrier between her and the rest of the train.

She took a shuddering breath. "I was looking for Maj."

"I know." He ignored her raised eyebrow. They could discuss more on that later. "We can help you find her, but—"

"We?"

"Luke is back on one of the other cars. We can help you, but first tell me why you were running?"

"I was afraid you would think that I helped my uncle and Weldon. You would have every reason to believe that."

"Possibly. I had to consider it, Kirsten. I hope you understand that. No matter that it tore me apart, I had to think it possible. It's my job."

She shook her head. "One thing I have learned about you, Simon, is that it's more than your job; it's who you are."

He gave her a crooked smile. That was true. She wasn't the only one to note it.

"So, what made you think that I'm not involved? Or aren't you sure?"

"You have to understand, Kirsten, I have very, very good instincts, and they told me you were innocent. But the full confession that Luke received from your uncle and fiancé clinched the matter." He used the term purposely, and wasn't disappointed. He watched her clench her jaw before she spoke, spitting out the words.

"Don't call him that. He was never that and you know it."

He let his breath out in a whoosh. "So you never loved him?" He had to hear those words from her kissable lips.

"I never loved him—I didn't even like him! I only went along with it in the beginning because it seemed to please my uncle and I do owe him so much."

"Perhaps. But you don't owe Weldon anything."

"No, I don't. Perhaps if I had loved him it would have been different."

He didn't want to hear that. He abruptly changed the subject. "How did you plan to find your sister?"

"There's nothing for me in Hobart anymore, so I decided that I would look for newspaper jobs, even stringers, in different places and try to track her that way. Someone will have noticed if she has come through. I know she was heading east."

Does she have much money? Do you think she'll go straight through to wherever she's headed?"

"I don't know, Simon. That's part of the problem. I thought I would stay in Star Junction for a day or so, and move on."

Simon frowned. "That doesn't seem enough time to do a story."

"Not this time, no. I have enough money to get me to Normalville. I plan to spend a week there before moving on."

Simon covered her hand with his. "Let me help. Luke will want to help too."

She raised startled eyes to his. "What can you do differently?"

Simon grinned at her. "You would be amazed. Now, Luke and I have some vacation time coming. I don't see any problem in using it after we get to Washington."

"You're still going?" Disappointment colored her voice. "I thought maybe you would be able to help me now." She straightened in her seat and gave a slight chuckle. "I'm being nonsensical."

Squeezing her hand, he said, "I'm sorry, it's my job, Kirsten. I gave my oath that I would uphold the government; this is part of it."

"I understand."

"Do you?" He gripped her hands in both of his, squeezing, looking into her eyes and seeing the truth of what she said.

"Of course I do! When you love someone, you tend to be aware of those things." She bit her lip, but didn't turn away.

"Do you mean that?" He hoped the intensity of his voice, his whole being, didn't turn her away.

"I do, but it's all right." She slipped one of her hands from beneath his and caressed his cheek. "I am a big girl, you know, and I realize that one can't always help the way they feel." She let her hand drop to his shoulder, then to her lap. "I'm sure I'll get over it."

"What if I don't?" He watched her eyes widen as her gaze met his. He reached to cup her cheek, and let his hand tunnel through the back of her hair, loosening it further. She reached up a hand and rested it on his arm, stopping him. She would have spoken, but raising his other hand, he placed his finger on her lips. "I love you, Kirsten. That has been the biggest problem in this whole investigation."

He leared closer to kiss her, then heard Luke's voice. "So, you found her!"

Simon leaned his forehead against Kirsten's and chuckled, then straightened. "You know Luke is my partner?" he asked her.

"Yes."

Simon waved his hand between them. "That means we're practically a package deal." Seeing the puzzlement in her eyes, he clarified. "Marry me, and you have to put up with him. A lot."

"Marry. .marry?"

Luke leaned against the seat and started chuckling. "How many times have I told you, Sime. No one is a mind reader. Did you remember to actually ask her?"

"Umm... That may have slipped my mind. Why don't you go sit down?" he said to Luke, and promptly turned his back on him.

This time, he leaned to whisper his question in her ear.

Author's Note:

1874 was an exciting time for America. Aside from adjustments to becoming the United States, there was expansion to the west, and a railroad system that could get you from one coast to the other in seven days.

While Simon and Luke are fictional characters, they're positions were very real. The creation of the Secret Service was the last official act of President Lincoln, signed only hours before his death. The Secret Service at the time was not as we think of it today. Created on July 5, 1865, its role was to suppress counterfeit currency. According to Secret Service history, it wasn't until 1867 that their responsibilities included "detecting persons perpetrating frauds against the government."

One thing I found very difficult to write, was when Simon or Luke needed to identify themselves. I was so tempted to provide identification, but the first commission book and a new badge was not issued to operatives until 1875.

I thoroughly enjoyed writing about Simon and Kirsten, and Luke and Maj. I hope you found their world as exciting as I did.

ABOUT THE AUTHOR

Always a daydreamer, author Tara Manderino loves to create stories and situations for the people running around in her head. She first began writing in third grade when she realized she couldn't afford her reading habit.

She writes and is published in a variety of genres and finds that each one is her favorite at the time.

Tara resides in her native town in southwestern Pennsylvania. When she's not chasing Lydia, the boxer, she's writing her own stories, or reading, Tara likes to bake, watch old movies, and do a variety of crafts.

www.ingramcontent.com/pod-product-compliance
Lightning Source LLC
Chambersburg PA
CBHW051819170626
46807CB00003B/944